She stood, her breath suspended with fright, staring at the dark spots beneath the curtain.

There was a blur of swaying drapery, then a large pair of shoulders moved swiftly in the faint light from the window to place themselves behind her. He had been there all the time, hiding behind the curtain to attack her. He had even watched her change her clothing.

"Don't make a sound. I have a gun," Kiley said softly in her ear. "I'm not going to hurt you. I just want the letter. Where is it?"

Fawcett Books
by Joan Smith:

PRELUDE TO LOVE

JOAN SMITH

FAWCETT CREST • NEW YORK

A Fawcett Crest Book
Published by Ballantine Books

Library of Congress Catalog Card Number: 82-90858

ISBN 0-449-20092-2

Manufactured in the United States of America

First Ballantine Books Edition: March 1983

CHAPTER
One

"*I*F YOUR PAPA suggests *one more* utterly stupid and unnecessary chore for us to do today, Nessie, I shall screech," Miss Simons declared, with a dangerous flash of her faded blue eyes. "Wrapping the silver flatware in oilskin and burying it under the floorboards! What can *possibly* be the point of it? And what are we to eat our mutton with in the meanwhile?"

"Everyone is hiding his valuables," Vanessa pointed out, but with very little enthusiasm. "In the meanwhile, we shall use the tinware from the kitchen. Come, let us get it done as quickly as possible, so that we can get back to my gown."

Together the two ladies, aunt and niece, laboriously wrapped each individual spoon, knife and fork in oilskin, the whole to be placed in a wooden tea crate and hidden under the floor, to keep it safe when the French invaded. The sooner it was done, the sooner they could return to their interrupted chore of sewing spangles on the white *peau de soie* underskirt of Miss Bradford's ball gown. This latter job had to be finished by the next evening, for the military ball was fast approaching.

The whole east coast of England was busy hiding valuable possessions from Napoleon, whose arrival on England's shore was considered imminent. What items were not concealed were packed up in carriages, ready to be taken to safety with the occupants when the great evacuation occurred. There was scarcely an elegant home in the neighborhood whose walls were not denuded of paintings, and whose table bore real silver. Attics, cellars and secret passages were where these items were now to be found. Mrs. Whistler had her entire Sèvres tea service put down the well in a wooden bucket, while the Delons had gone through their famous library to sort out the valuable editions and hide them in the church, boarded up under the bench of their family pew.

"I hope he doesn't take into his head to make us bury our jewels," Miss Simons rattled on. "It will be the last straw if you cannot wear your mama's diamonds to the ball. How else should you attract Colonel Forrester?"

Vanessa lifted her eyes to the mirror on the far wall to assess her other attractions. She gazed with satisfaction on a crown of golden curls, cut fashionably short to frame her young face. Her eyes, green, large and lustrous, she thought might work some charm on Forrester, if only he could ever get close enough to appreciate them. The length and thickness of her lashes could not really be done justice from across the street, which was the minimum distance usually placed between Forrester and herself.

Colonel Forrester was the commandant of the garrison that had sprung up on the coast, ready to repulse Napoleon's attack. He was every inch the fine officer—tall, handsome, well mannered and, best of all, not averse to a flirtation. He was seen on the strut in the village, sitting as straight and stiff as a statue in his scarlet regimentals in church on Sunday, but it was generally agreed amongst the young ladies that he showed to best advantage mounted on his fine Bay mare, riding amongst the tents that had grown up in such delightful profusion along the coast between Hastings and Eastbourne. To see his underlings jump to attention, saluting and hopping to obey his orders, filled their hearts with joy. It was difficult to take the threat of

Napoleon Bonaparte seriously when there was a Colonel Forrester standing by to protect them. Vanessa had first thought he would be frequently in the Bradford saloon, for her father was a retired colonel, but it had not proved the case. He had come once to pay his respects, and had his handsome ears burned for the dilatory manner in which he was preparing his defenses. He had come no more. Her father had offended him to such a degree that he did no more than bow, very stiffly, when they met in the village.

She knew the ball was her only chance to attract him. Forrester had hired the assembly hall in the village to toss a major ball, as a reward for his men's long vigil there on the coast. It was to be such a social event as rarely occurred in the quiet lives of the locals. Hundreds of officers were to come, from as far away as Portsmouth and Margate. Elaborate preparations were going forth at the assembly rooms, turning them into some exotic setting. Discussing these decorations, arranging their toilettes and discovering the names of the officers coming from afar had made up the main topic of conversation amongst the ladies for several weeks now. Miss Fischer had sent off to London to have her jewelry returned from safekeeping there. Miss Fischer, a lively brunette heiress, was the main contender for Colonel Forrester's hand.

It *did* seem hard that Vanessa must content herself with the company of mere majors or captains, or even platoon lieutenants, when a perfectly eligible colonel was to be had. He was not entirely averse to her green eyes either. He cast surreptitious glances in her direction when they met, but was shy to put himself forward after the scorching tirade her father had submitted him to during his one visit to Levenhurst. He had been known to say to Miss Condie that he feared Miss Bradford had a low opinion of him. Really it was enough to cast a girl into the dismals to consider it. Low opinion indeed! But at least her father did not plan to attend the ball. Next evening she would have the opportunity to correct Colonel Forrester's misapprehension about her feelings.

"I shall wear my diamonds," Vanessa said. "They are not buried, but locked in the trunk of Army papers Papa has got packed in his carriage to be taken away when—*if* we have to evacuate. Do you think we will, Auntie?''

Miss Simons clucked unhappily at the question. She preferred not to consider life's unpleasant side. She had more important matters weighing on her small mind. Should she have the large spangles sewed on Nessie's underskirt, or select smaller ones to go on top? Ought she to snip another quarter of an inch from the girl's curls today, or should this major surgery wait till after the ball? There was no saying with a new haircut; it might turn out superbly, but on the other hand, newly-cut hair was often recalcitrant, sitting out at odd and unattractive angles.

Nor was her niece's toilette the only matter to be considered. She had no notion of appearing dowdy herself. Though half a century old, she was always spectacularly elegant. Even to wrap silver in oilskin, she wore a fine green sarsenet gown with a crisp white fichu, highlighted by a silver filigree brooch. Her dark hair, distinguished by two white wings at the temples, was arranged in a seemingly casual fashion that took forever to achieve. Her measurements were still those of her girlhood. She ate little and exercised much, her physical activity generally taking the form of running from house to house in the neighborhood, discovering what petty schemes, spites and feuds were brewing between friends. As often as Colonel Bradford allowed, Vanessa accompanied her aunt on these outings.

''If an invasion really is likely, we should go up to London,'' Miss Simons stated hopefully. ''It would be nice if Napoleon would hold off till the spring. The fall little season is not at all so fine as the spring. *I* made my bows in May. You ought by rights to have done the same, but your papa . . .'' She did not complete her statement. They both knew well enough what the colonel thought of such frivolity.

''He is not well enough to undertake the exertions of a Season,'' Vanessa explained, quite unnecessarily. It was no secret the colonel had been returned home from India owing to a chest wound that still bothered him considerably.

''He would not have to come,'' Aunt Elleri said quickly. "Indeed we would go on *much better* without him, to insult all the gentlemen. He always takes it amiss that an able-bodied gentleman is not in uniform. As to calling that nice Colonel Forrester a frivolous dandy! I cringe and blush every time I think of it. His mama the daughter of a viscount. But then, what is to be expected of a father who *beats* his daughter?"

There was little enough closeness between the father and daughter, but she could not hear him disparaged without defending him. "He does not beat me. It was only a spanking, years ago, when I was a child."

"*Only* a spanking! You are generous. I shall *never* forget the tears welling up in your eyes and coursing down your cheeks. To beat an innocent child, hardly more than a baby! It is the military influence. It removes all sense of decency from a man if he does not beware. It is really a wonder how Colonel Forrester has retained his sense of refinement. It is his never having had to fight yet that accounts for it, very likely. There would be many like him in London, *refined* officers, who wear the uniform but perform mainly ornamental functions."

"Yes, what Papa calls tin soldiers," Vanessa answered with a smile. "But there is no point speaking of London. We cannot abandon my father when he is ill. He needs us."

"Pooh!" was the answer to this filial statement. "That disreputable batman, Parkins, is the only one he allows to tend him. There—we are out of oilskin, thank God. I shall have to nip into the village and buy some more. Come along with me, Nessie. No, you had better stay home and apply that bleaching lotion I have decocted. It is fermenting on the windowsill of my room. *Excellent* for the complexion."

"Oh, but it is *green*, Auntie."

"Of course it is green, goose. It is the cucumber pulp that makes it so."

"I cannot even wander about the house if I put it on. Someone might call. Miss Condie, or Miss Fischer . . ."

"Not a chance of it. They will be walking the streets in the village, the trollops, trying for a sight of Forrester. He is bound to be there this afternoon, I should think, with the decoration of the assembly hall to be seen to. Perhaps you had better come with me. You can apply the lotion this evening. We will not have any callers this evening. The whole world will stay at home to prepare for the ball. We can remain in our rooms and finish your gown.''

''I had better see first if there is anything Papa wants in the village,'' Vanessa said, not eagerly, but as one willing to do her duty.

Miss Simons shook her head at this pandering to authority. Her niece returned ten minutes later, her shoulders sagging and her lips turned down. ''I can't go with you,'' she said. ''Papa wants me to oversee the packing of a cart for the servants. Dry foodstuffs and blankets, pots and pans. Oh, and you are to order a hundredweight of flour and a hundredweight of dried, salted fish, to be delivered as quickly as possible, to go in the servants' cart. Two dozen of candles, the tallow candles as well. Put it on his bill.''

''Pest of a man,'' Miss Simons scolded. ''Am I to waste my entire afternoon in the grocer's shop? I want to call on Mrs. Fischer. I know she is planning a dinner party before the ball. I thought she might invite us if she knew we are not having any party ourselves. It is very odd she did not ask us. You don't suppose she has inveigled Colonel Forrester to attend? That would make it imperative for him to stand up first with Clara, the lanky old hen.''

''Papa has asked the minister and Sir Charles Newcombe to dine here,'' Vanessa replied, with a vexed expression that did not know whether it was angry or grieved.

''An ancient church minister and a married man? It is all of a piece,'' Miss Simons exploded. There was no confusion in her sentiments. She was out of reason cross with her brother-in-law. Henry Bradford was doing his utmost to ruin Nessie's chances of ever making a good match. If he did not find some excuse at the last minute to forbid her attending the ball, it was more than she dared to hope for.

''I have to go now,'' Vanessa said, adopting a pout. ''Where are the winter blankets stored, Auntie?''

''In a chest in the spare room, the small green room at

the end of the hall. They will have to be put out to air. I packed them in camphor, against the moths. Be sure to wear a sunbonnet, Nessie. We don't want you cropping out in freckles for the ball. Lemons—I must ask cook to bring us some lemons. I shall double the lemon juice in my decoction. Wear your gloves too, when you are having the blankets hung. I shall go on into town and discover whether the Fischers are having a dinner party, and whether they have trapped Forrester into attending. They are so sly I place no reliance on their behaving properly in the matter.''

"Proper behavior" would leave Forrester for Vanessa, at least for the opening minuet. But there, the whole world was out to hamper the match. If the thing were to be pulled off, it would be herself who did it. She went to get her bonnet, to do battle with the world. Vanessa went to the green room to haul out the blankets and take her ill humor out on the servants. After she was actually out in the yard, wearing those defenses against Sol which her aunt advised, she was seduced into a softer frame of mind by the warming breezes and gently swaying trees. Her thoughts had soon wafted off to dream about being in the colonel's arms, hearing his excuses for being less particular in his attentions to herself than he wanted. She stared with distracted, unseeing eyes as the blankets were hung. How should she bother with blankets, when Colonel Forrester was proposing marriage to her, between impassioned embraces and declarations of undying love?

CHAPTER
Two

COLONEL BRADFORD, LATELY retired from His Royal
Majesty's Army with a chest wound contracted during
the battle of Assaye, in India, was extremely frustrated.
He was annoyed to see his only daughter, a once-
intelligent girl, had turned into a simpering miss, her
head full of nothing but beaux, balls and gowns. This
was a minor, daily irritation; his great frustration was
his physical condition. After seeing active duty against
the French forces in the Netherlands, the Americans in
the Colonies, and the Marathas in India, it was demmed
hard that he must be retired when a chance for glory
rested on his own doorstep. On a clear day, he could
see through his powerful telescope across the twenty-
five-mile Channel to Boulogne, where the armies of
Napoleon Bonaparte moved about, looking like a colony
of ants from that distance, but with the glitter of a
gun or bayonet picked out when the sun struck at the
proper angle. One hundred and fifty thousand men were
assembled, first making up the flat-bottomed boats from
green lumber just cut for the purpose, then performing their

maneuvers, and waiting for the weather to favor an attack on England.

The man London had seen fit to put in charge of the country's defense was another source of infinite frustration. Colonel Forrester was a green officer, whose experience was limited to parading up and down in front of St. James's Palace. Had Forrester at least been of a lower rank, he might have been amenable to direction, but he was a colonel, like himself. He had taken his duties seriously enough at first, but after some months of waiting, Forrester had become bored and turned socialite. His time was spent in courting the local girls, arranging parades for their amusement, and most recently, a ball. Bradford had done what he could—taken over the running of the local volunteer brigade, but he knew a group of civilians with pikes and turnip sticks were not going to hold Bonaparte off for long.

He had his scouts set up on the highest point of the coast, twenty-four hours a day, with their two ricks, one of furze, to burst into flame at once, the other of turf, for a longer light. They were to be fired instantly at the first sight of the flat boats' approach. The ricks' firing was a signal to ring the church bells in a prearranged order, to assemble the volunteers. It was also the signal for the women, older men and children to run for their carriages and carts, wherein were assembled sufficient foods and blankets to ease their flight inland. He had seen, in foreign lands, the chaos, the panic that resulted from a lack of such essential preparation. Yet it was hard to convince the local citizens to make ready, when his own family made a joke of it, and when Forrester broadcast his simple-minded views.

The green colonel outlined in minute detail the conditions under which Boney would strike. There was to be a twenty-four-hour fog, accompanied by a dead calm, to enable the flat-bottomed boats to be oared across, while English sailing ships were becalmed. Forrester spoke vaguely of a spring tide as well, to hasten the charge. As spring was now past, the vigil had been relaxed. The men at the garrison had decided to dance the summer away, it seemed.

Bradford was not well, but he was not totally incapacitated, by a long shot. Many a dark night he went alone, or with his silent, sharp-eyed batman, Parkins, to the cliff to see the guards were awake at their ricks. This done, he would continue down the coast if the night was foggy, to listen and peer into the mist, his ears cocked for the sound of French accents. He knew every foot of the coast for ten miles in either direction. From Tyne in the far north down the east coast and around the corner to Wight and even west to Land's End, watches were kept around the clock, but it was at Boulogne the army was preparing, and anyone but a nodcock must know that with flat-bottomed boats, it was a straight shot across the Channel that was to be expected.

Bradford's own defenses were concentrated between Dungeness and Eastbourne. Rye was a possibility—the French had hit there in 1377, as any student of military history knew. Unfortunately, Forrester was not aware of military history. He had his troops clustered farther south. Bradford knew all the possible landing spots, and knew too that Boney was minutely aware of where Forrester's armies were gathered. He would not attack too close to them, yet the oared boats restricted him to a limited stretch of coast. When all his thinking was done, Bradford came to realize his own stretch of coast, just below Hastings, was as likely a spot as any. It thrilled him, to think he might stand with a rifle in his hands on his own land and repel the French invasion. Ha, there was more than one way to become a general! That would do it, retired or not.

The colonel could not sleep. He had moved his chamber to the front of the house to give him a view of the coast, but the view tonight was poor, due to a fog that hovered out at sea, and crept in to shift about the corners of the house. On such a night as this, the ricks might be fired, and the church bells rung. But if the French came, Bradford was not of a mind to learn it from the bells, which would be a half hour after the first onslaught. He felt a queer, tingling sensation along the back of his spine. A hardened veteran, he had more than once been saved from death by harking to these instinctive warnings. He arose silently, and without striking a light, shuffled into his buckskins and jacket, struggled with his top boots, wondering whether to rouse Parkins for the job. It bothered his chest, to have to yank and pull them on himself. No, let the fellow sleep, for it was likely all a sleeveless errand, this quick dash down to the sea, to listen once again for the splash of French oars. He had learned that a French oar was indistinguishable from an English one. Oftimes he had stood with his heart hammering, his finger cocked on the trigger of his pistol, only to hear the familiar dull voice of the local fishermen, complaining of the cold and damp, or the paucity of their catch.

The night was dark and eerie, with a light wind soughing through the trees. There was a sudden flutter of wings as a great owl darted from a tree to catch an unwary nocturnal animal. A terrified squeal signified the owl's success, then silence descended again. He walked on, down to the shingle beach, looking and listening while the waves lapped at his feet. The beacons on the hill were not visible from here. No matter, the lads couldn't see anything in this fog in any case. Boney might come tonight or tomorrow night or any night, and Forrester would be lying in a drunken stupor, or sitting in some lady's saloon. He pulled out his watch, reading with difficulty the hour was three-thirty. Nonsense. He'd go home to his warm bed. He was tired, with that old ache in the chest that limited his labors so severely. Seeing a large rock in his path, he sat on it to catch his breath.

Then he heard it, the telltale lapping of oars, out of rhythm with the louder lapping of the sea. As often as he had heard it, his heart still quickened. Listening more intently, he realized it was only one boat, and relaxed. Not the invasion, then. It might be smugglers, which was of interest only inasmuch as he hoped for a safe delivery. He liked his brandy very well. The boat, to his surprise, was landed, pulled with a quiet rasp up on the shingle beach. He was about to arise and make himself known when he heard a man say in a very low voice, "*Que penses-tu?*" He sat rigid, every nerve taut. Frenchmen! He could not see them, and assumed that he was equally obscured by the heavy fog. "*Pas trop mal, hein?*"

A second man replied, also in French, but was understood by the colonel, who numbered French amongst his accomplishments. They were only two—youngish men, from their voices. The next speech brought the colonel to rigid attention.

"Looks like a good spot to me," the other man answered. "We'll scout farther along and see if there's any defense. Our general thinks not, but who can trust spies of any nationality?"

"Easy landing," the first speaker pointed out, the whole talk in French.

"Yes, but where the devil *are* we?"

"That place with the lights just northward must have been Hastings. We're a few miles from it. I'll go this way, you that. One of us is bound to meet our contact. We'll meet back here in an hour. If he says all is quiet here, no troops or guns in the immediate area, we shall suggest this spot to the general."

"A pity he hung back. We could have taken the *anglais* easily enough tonight, no?"

"You forget we wait for General Vachon and his men to join us from La Rochelle. It won't be before two weeks. Be careful."

They separated. Not even a shadow in the fog showed their routes. Bradford sat frozen to his rock, willing himself to silent invisibility. He heard their stealthy steps recede, and knew he had gone undetected. After a safe interval, he crept to the boat and searched it, but wasted very little time on this instinctive chore. They were not bringing messages or hiding plans in their small boat. Impossible to credit they had made the crossing in it. No, they had come most of the way in a larger ship, certainly. And now one of them was going to meet a spy. He longed to learn the traitor's identity, but with two to follow, and with the fog to shroud them, it was difficult. He knew too that he was an old, disabled man. If he were found out, this precious information he had gleaned would be lost forever to England. His first duty was to get himself to safety, and the information to London. The name Forrester occurred to him, only to be rejected. He did not wish to have this priceless news treated as a joke, the hallucination of a quack, or worse, publicly discussed amongst the officers. It must be quickly delivered to the ears of some highly placed, trusted man in power, perhaps the secretary of state for war. A soldier himself, he had an innate mistrust of politicians, and sought about in his mind for another recipient of the news. He settled on Sir Giles Harkman, an ex-general turned privy councillor, a man he had served under in India and a trusted friend. He was now attached to the War Office in some capacity, which made him eminently suitable.

He hastened home at a pace that threatened his heart. He was gasping as he got through the great double doors of Levenhurst, to drag himself up the broad oaken staircase and fall onto his bed, exhausted. He lay for a quarter of an hour, catching his breath, and making plans to go to London at once with his important message. At the end of that time, he doubted he could even get out of his own clothing without Parkins' help, much less go to London. Perhaps he would feel stouter by morning. He would rest till dawn, and see whether it improved his condition.

He was still asleep when Parkins peeped his head into the room the next morning, to enquire in a condemnatory tone what he was about, sleeping in his jacket and boots.

Bradford considered informing Parkins of his discovery, then decided to keep it to himself. He ordered a valise packed and the horses put to for a drive to London.

"Not if *I* know anything, you're not going to be jostled to death in a carriage!" Parkins said sternly, staring up from his five feet three inches of wiry strength into the towering face of his master. "Wheezing, you are, and if you haven't got a chill, out prowling them beaches in the dark of night and sleeping without a blanket thrown over your body, it's more than *I* know."

Bradford prepared to set his batman down, but was seized with a bout of coughing that pained his chest badly. When it was over, he sank, weak and panting, on the side of his bed, perfectly aware that he was in no shape to deliver the message himself. He'd have to send Parkins. He ordered breakfast in his chamber, along with writing materials. While he ate toast and sipped tea, he wrote out in precise detail for the eyes of Sir Giles Harkman exactly what he had experienced the night before. Then, with a somewhat malicious smile, he went on to outline the mis-management that was taking place under Colonel Forrester's command. He had been itching to do it for a long time, had restrained himself only out of a sense of respect for a fellow officer, and the fear of not being taken seriously. Imminent invasion was of sufficient importance to make his task a pleasant duty.

In an accelerating rush of enthusiasm, he went on to outline his own plans, filling two sheets with closely writ-ten lines. He folded them into an envelope, applied hot wax and stamped his seal on it. His daily mail was brought up as he finished this job. He recognized Sir Giles' own writing in the small pile of letters, and pulled it out eagerly. The two ex-campaigners kept in fairly close con-tact by correspondence. The letter informed him that Sir Giles was taking a short respite from his duties, at his home in Ipswich, a hard two-days' drive from Levenhurst. London could be reached in one. This set Bradford frown-ing in distress. Harkman was the perfect man to tell his news to. The invasion was far enough in the future that the extra day could be spared. The next problem was that he was not well enough to part with Parkins for four full days—two there and two back. Feeling poorly, as he did, he needed this pair of legs to look after him, and to oversee the volunteer brigade's activities.

He sat considering who to send in his stead. A mad dash from the Bradford household might alert the spies in the neighborhood to the nature of the trip, and cause interfer-ence. In particular, he feared the unknown spy who had met the Frenchmen the night before. Having selected Brad-ford's very doorstep as the invasion spot, it was logical the man was keeping a sharp eye on himself. But his daughter and her aunt—who would ever suspect two tame ladies of being involved in anything serious? Nothing would be suspected if Miss Bradford should go to visit her friend

Lady Harkman for a week. It would be taken for a mere social visit. She must leave immediately to be halfway to Maidstone before anyone knew she was gone. In that way, it was impossible she should be overtaken. Balls played so small a part in the colonel's life that he was only vaguely aware of the pending ball, did not even realize it was to occur that same evening. Vanessa was called to his chamber for instructions.

CHAPTER
Three

VANESSA AWOKE THAT morning with a heady feeling of excitement. *At last* the long-awaited day had come! Papa was not at all biddable in allowing her to attend social functions at the military base, but a ball in the assembly rooms had miraculously been permitted. Her eyes flew to the gown hanging on the back of her door, the filmy white confection with the large spangles now all in place on the underskirt. She had gone to bed with the cucumber lotion on not only her face, but her hands as well, which were covered by old white cotton gloves to save the sheets from stains. She hopped up, removing the gloves to see what miracle they had wrought. The only miracle was that the cotton had absorbed the lotion. She lifted the hem of her skirt, admiring the dainty apple-green velvet ribbon used for trim. A length of the same ribbon would be wound through her curls, to match her eyes. A pair of green kid slippers sat on the floor, looking ready to start dancing by themselves.

She glanced to the window, where the sun, a relative stranger here on the coast, beamed through the leaded panes, promising a gorgeous day. She would risk her complexion in a brisk ride in the morning—go to Miss Condie's home and confirm that the Fischers were having Forrester and two majors to dinner. Mrs. Fischer had withheld the news from Aunt Elleri, but the whole village was buzzing with it. In the afternoon she would lie down for two hours to ensure that her eyes sparkled as hard as everyone else's at the dance, then she would have her hair done up in papers, have a bath and begin the final stage of preparations.

It was not often she had a day of such unparalleled pleasure to consider, here in the quiet countryside. She hoped Papa would do nothing to spoil it. She was not so well acquainted with her father as most daughters are, owing to his absence during her growing up. He was always away at some war or other. She knew him mainly from letters, till two years ago, when he had come home, a cranky invalid. A further blow had been added by her mother's death soon afterwards—a sad irony that his wife should have died so soon after his return. It almost seemed he blamed *her* for it. He had not been so ill-humored before becoming a widower. Mama could always laugh and tease him into humor, but lately he did nothing but jaw at her for being a vain, frivolous, silly girl, and at Aunt Elleri for adding to her vanity.

There was a tap at her door. Without waiting for an answer, Elleri Simons came tripping in, elegant in a pale mauve morning gown, her coiffure already in exquisite place. As her chief interest in life was elegance, her first thought was to examine the gown for flaws. She knew, of course, that an invasion was often spoken of, but any thought she spent on it was to wonder how one addressed a French general, and whether he should be asked to tea.

"Good morning, dear," she said gaily over her shoulder. "I have had the most *ravishing* idea. The new issue of the *Belle Assemblée* is here. I want to get at your hair at once. I shall do it in the *chérubin* for the ball. I must nip off the bits over the ears, and do it up in papers."

"Oh, Auntie, you cut it last week. Please don't take any more off, or I shall look like a boy."

"That is exactly the point, pet. Only an inch, I promise you. After you see the model in the magazine you will *know* I am right. It will be divine. As soon as you have seen your papa I shall do it. Come to me as soon as you have eaten breakfast. But of course you must see your papa first. He is asking for you. If he means to cancel the ball, I shall be ill. *Don't* let him do it. Promise him anything—that you won't speak to Colonel Forrester, or stand up with him, or do a thing but run him down." Her eyes turned back to the gown. "I wonder if we were right to stay with the large spangles. I have the smaller ones in my room, but to remove these and put the others on will take the newness out of the material. It *does* soften it, so much handling. But we'll decide later. You had better see your papa and be sure we *are* to attend the ball."

"He couldn't be so mean!"

"I'm sure he would not, but he has had the horses put to, and whatever can he have done *that* for? *He* is not well enough to go anywhere, and it is the old traveling carriage that is being washed down."

With an expression of the utmost fright, Vanessa threw on her dressing gown and hurried out the door. She burst into his room, wearing a worried frown.

"Don't worry, my dear, I am not dying," her father said, in a comforting way. "I expect the servants have frightened you half to death."

She noticed then that he was paler than usual, his face bearing traces of his suffering, in the deep lines that gouged ruts from nose to chin. She felt sorry for him, and some remorse for her selfishness. It must be horrid to be an old man, sick and unable to enjoy any of life's pleasures. It was enough to put anyone out of humor. "You look pale, Papa. Can I do something for you?"

"It happens you can," he said, and went on to outline what was demanded of her. All her sympathy and remorse evaporated. He was doing it on purpose to make her miss the ball.

"But I *can't* go today, Papa!" she exclaimed.

"You can and must," he told her, not stridently, but very firmly.

"What can be so important it cannot wait till tomorrow?"

"The letter you are to deliver to Sir Giles for me. Don't ask what it contains. I am not at liberty to divulge it to just anyone. You must take my word for it the matter is of great importance and great urgency. You will drive as hard as you can, stopping only when necessary. Don't speak to anyone—that is, I would not like you to act in any *suspicious* manner. Behave as though you were going for a social visit, but do it with all speed. Stay overnight at good inns, but be up and leave early in the morning. I cannot foresee any danger in it for you, if you leave promptly and set a hot pace. No one will know you are gone till you have driven safely beyond catching up. Speed and discretion—I cannot impress their necessity on you too strongly."

"Just one more day, Papa," she said, disheartened. "Tomorrow . . ."

"Don't make me ashamed for you, Vanessa," he said. "You are singularly fortunate in being chosen to perform one worthwhile act in your worthless life. Do it with pride and pleasure. Much depends on it. I say with regret that I would not entrust this mission to you if I had anyone else I might send."

"Parkins could . . ."

"My decision has been made," he said. "Leave, as quickly as you can throw your linens into a valise."

She returned to her room, her bottom lip quivering, a tear forming in her eyes. She cast a loathsome glance at the letter to Sir Giles Harkman. It was all a hoax, an excuse to keep her from Colonel Forrester. Oh, it was *cruel!*

Miss Simons awaited her, still examining the gown. "We have put on too many velvet bows," she decreed, mentally selecting those for removal. "The spangles we shall leave as they are."

"By all means leave the gown as it is, for I shan't be wearing it. We are not going to the ball," Vanessa said, her voice grim.

"My pet! You cannot mean it!"

"I have an errand to perform for Papa. A most urgent

errand, you understand. A letter for Sir Giles. You are to come with me, Auntie, so you had better pack a nightgown into a valise. We are to leave within the half hour, sooner if possible."

"Half an hour! I couldn't be ready for a week. For London one requires . . ."

"Sir Giles is at home in Ipswich."

"Ipswich? You are mad, or your papa is. No one goes to Ipswich. I should not mind going to London tomorrow, after the ball. The Season is spent, but with autumn coming on, it would be amusing."

"We are not going for amusement; it is only to be a *social* call if anyone happens to enquire."

"What is in this marvelous letter?" Elleri asked, her eyes narrowing.

"Business. Military business, I suppose. A matter of the utmost importance. We are to guard it with our lives."

There was a good deal of excited chatter, taking up ten minutes of the allowed thirty before they were to leave. The colonel came along to his daughter's room to hasten her departure, and to give more instructions for the disposal of the letter.

"Tuck it into the front of your gown," he suggested. "And don't let it out of your hands, even when you are sleeping."

"Can't you tell me what is in it?"

He considered doing so, but as Miss Simons chose that moment to stick her head in at the door, he hastily reconsidered. "Be sure to take an extra pair of kid gloves, Nessie. Gloves always become smudged on a journey," Miss Simons said.

Nessie would in all likelihood tell that rattlepate of a woman what the message was. He could not trust Elleri Simons as far as he could throw a house. "I can't, but you may be sure of its importance, Nessie. I have to speak to Parkins now. Don't waste a moment."

Her father turned to leave, then spotted her new ball gown, hanging on the door. "Sorry about your missing the dance. I see you have had a new gown made up. You shall wear it when you return—at your own ball. I'll give you a fine ball here at Levenhurst, Nessie, as a reward. Ask who you like to it." This was oblique permission to include the detested young colonel.

Her old remorse returned to plague her. Papa was *not* depriving her of the dance on purpose. That the letter contained any message vital to the safety of the country, she could not believe for a moment, but that her father thought so, she reluctantly accepted. She went to the door and placed a kiss on his cheek. "Thank you, Papa. That will be lovely."

He patted her hand, feeling a twinge of conscience that he did the proper thing, to send his helpless daughter on so dangerous a mission. "Be very careful."

"I will, Papa."

"Of course you will. You are your father's daughter, after all," he consoled himself.

After he left, Vanessa tried to stick a thick letter into the bosom of a lightweight sprigged muslin gown. Its four corners stuck out, calling more attention to it than Papa would care for, or than was quite comfortable for herself. She held it in her hands a moment, looking around for a better place to hide it. She had a small valise on her bed, the only case she intended taking. Elleri came into the room again. "The letter would be safer in the large trunk, would it not?" she asked.

"We are not taking a large trunk. There isn't time to pack one."

"It is half packed, goose. Go to Ipswich without a trunk? You are mad. Give me the letter."

"No, I'll keep it," she said, putting it into her small valise and folding a spare petticoat on top of it. "We had better go now."

"I shall be ready in two minutes," Elleri said casually, then went back to her room to sort in a leisurely fashion through her gowns, selecting one, and pushing another aside. She trotted back and forth, down the hall, reminding her charge to pack extra stockings, for a stocking was bound to poke out a toe on a trip; to bring her own soap—there was nothing but lye soap to be had at an inn, and a dozen other non-necessities, till the trunk was filled to the brim. When the servants took the trunk down, her aunt even picked up a glass-faced traveling clock, framed in brass, with a ring on top to aid carrying.

"We would not want to be without a clock in the carriage," she said. "Handsome, is it not? My father gave it to me when he died—in his will. I never travel without it."

Its handsome hands showed the half hour allowed by Colonel Bradford for their departure had doubled to an hour, and *still* they had not left.

Their exit down the front stairs was silent, to prevent his hearing at what time they were finally going. When they got in the carriage, Vanessa noticed that in all the confusion, she had worn her oldest slippers, blue ones that were so very comfortable but not at all stylish. Abovestairs, Bradford sat worrying that he should have sent some outriders with the ladies, but he did not wish to call any extraordinary attention to the vehicle, and hoped the groom and footman between them would follow his instructions. They had been told to go at top speed, changing teams as often as necessary, and hang the expense. Parkins had packed a brace of pistols under the box seat, after giving the groom a hasty lesson in how to use them.

Bradford ordered his batman to bring him a large pot of what he called Irish tea, which conveyed that milk was to be left out, and whiskey used instead. It was his favorite restorative in India, where milk had seemed to come curdled from the cows. While he sipped and worried and made more plans to counteract the invasion, the carriage pounded its way northward, causing much consternation in the hearts of the occupants. They were strongly inclined to have it stopped and jump out when they saw the number of scarlet jackets milling around town, in the vicinity of the assembly rooms. Major Rooney and Captain Schroeder, cantering past them, lifted their right hand in the quasi-military salute used to honor ladies.

"I wonder where Forrester is," Miss Simons said, giving voice to her companion's very thought.

"He is probably inside the rooms. They say the hall has been done up like a Persian tent for the night."

"I heard at Fischers yesterday he sent all the way to London for a dozen orange trees. The hall will be half full of greenery if they are right. But the Fischers exaggerate everything. How I should love to see it."

"Papa said to hurry," Nessa answered, but in her heart she was strongly inclined to add to her sorrow by seeing just a little of what she would be missing that night.

"Bother!" Miss Simons exclaimed suddenly. "I have forgotten to bring along my vinaigrette. I could not dream of undertaking a trip without one. I must have the carriage stopped," she said, already jerking on the check string. "As the assembly hall is only a step away, we might as well take a look in."

"With a glance at the traveling clock on the seat beside her, Vanessa knew they were behind schedule. She also suspected that had the assembly hall been located next the drapery shop, it would be stockings that were required, but she was not so convinced of her trip's urgency that she undertook to argue with her companion. The carriage was stopped. To satisfy the groom, she did indeed pick up a vinaigrette, but the ladies also went to have a look at the yards of pink and purple silk suspended from the ceiling of the assembly hall, tethered close to the floor with satin rope swags. The orange trees had just arrived. There was some confusion and good-natured bantering going forth amongst the officers who were in charge of distributing them along the wall. At the end of the hall stood a trestle table to be used for refreshments that night. It seemed hardly worth the stop—Forrester had not yet arrived. The scarlet jackets were gratifyingly eager to stop and chat, each wearer asking for a dance that night.

"You waste your breath, gentlemen. Miss Bradford will not be here," Miss Simons said. Vanessa nudged her elbow, trying to urge her to silence. Papa had not said to be quiet in front of the officers, but this was only because he never dreamed they would be so indiscreet as to stop at the village. An outcry was heard from the men, who had to hear why this was necessary.

"I am going to visit a friend," was all Vanessa said.

"Must you go today?" one officer demanded.

"This very moment," she said, drawing her aunt away.

Miss Simons tarried, her glance sliding often to the door to see if Forrester had come yet. At the edge of the group, one gentleman hung back. He was not in scarlet, but stood with a few civilians who were there to gawk. His face took on a look, first of sharp interest, then of suspicion, as he considered this sudden trip north by Colonel Bradford's daughter. It must be an important matter to take her away at such a time. He remembered his meeting on the beach the night before, and the crucial business discussed there. Was it possible Bradford had overheard them? As soon as the ladies left, he went to the inn where he was registered and called for his curricle. A curricle traveled at a faster pace than a carriage; he was in no fear of losing them. He would not overtake them before they stopped at an inn for the night. His dealings could not be executed on the King's highway in broad daylight, unless he wished to turn highwayman.

CHAPTER
Four

*T*HEY DROVE FOR four hours, stopping only once, to make a change of team, before continuing on to Maidstone, where they were to take lunch. Miss Simons hired a private parlor, where they could ease their bones in privacy from the merciless jostling of a carriage in a hurry. "I expect I should have had the letter taken out of the valise and brought in with me," Vanessa said with a twinge of conscience.

"I should not think it at all likely Boney's spies will root through your linens, my dear. They have better things to do," her aunt replied with a lifted brow.

"Papa *did* say to behave as though it were an ordinary trip, so perhaps it would be best not to call attention to the valise," Vanessa rationalized.

When eventually they went out, the valise was still strapped to the top of the carriage. "We took turns grabbing a bite so the carriage would never be abandoned," the groom whispered aside to Miss Bradford.

"Did you think that necessary?" she asked, wondering why it should be so, when the letter, for all they knew, was with herself.

"In case anyone should try to sabotage the carriage—smash up a wheel or axle," he explained. "Since we got a late start, we don't want to risk any more delays."

"No one tried such a thing?" she asked, becoming alarmed.

"No, no. Not with one of us there the whole time. You won't be dallying around town, ma'am?"

"We shall leave at once," Vanessa answered, concluding the servants were taking her errand more seriously than she was herself.

It was back on the road, for another long jolt all the way to Tilbury, before they stopped for the night. The shadows were lengthening, and while they might have covered a few more miles before darkness actually descended, Miss Simons announced, when she saw the signs of a town before her, that she would not travel another inch that day, if she carried in the letter word of an assassination attempt on the King himself. Vanessa too was weary, and agreed. As she got down from the carriage, her toe caught the edge of a cobblestone, and the sole of her old blue slipper pulled away a little from the upper.

"What a nuisance! And I haven't packed another pair. What shall I do, Auntie? This will be flapping and making it impossible for me to walk before we reach Ipswich."

"Take a run down the street and see if the cobbler's shop is open, while I hire us a room. What a shabby place it is, to be sure. The White Swan—no imagination. There is nothing but George's and Swan's and Greenmen from one end of the country to the other. Hurry, Nessie. We want to be sure of a private parlor."

"Gretch, will you personally look after my valise?" Vanessa said. She was embarrassed to tell him why. "My jewelry is in it," she said instead, to ensure his closest scrutiny.

"Nay, Miss Bradford. *I'll* go with you to the cobbler's, and Harrow will look after the valise," he told her. Gretch, the groom, was the senior servant, who felt it his duty to tend the letter.

She hesitated, wanting him to stay behind. "Now, miss, this is no time to be thinking I'm not fancy enough to go with you. You'd prefer Harrow's smart livery, I know, but your papa told *me* to guard you, and guard you I shall." He turned back to the footman. "Look sharp there, Harrow, to Miss Bradford's valise," he ordered before leaving.

After a hasty walk down the street, they found the cobbler's blinds drawn for the night. With a sigh, Vanessa looked at her slipper. It was not actually flapping. Only an inch had torn loose at the toe. "It will hold till we reach Ipswich," Gretch told her. "You won't be doing any walking."

By the time they returned to the White Swan, her aunt was waiting in the lobby. "Ah, good, you are here. Did you get it fixed?"

"No, it was closed. Pity."

"I don't know why you wore those old slippers in the first place, when you have your new patent ones that look much better. It is no matter; no one will see us. I have hired a private parlor, but want your opinion on our chambers for the night. They do not have two adjoining. They have two a mile apart, or one large, we might share. Which do you prefer?"

Vanessa, unaccustomed to public inns, had no desire to be pitched all alone into a room for the night. Neither was she eager to share a room with her talkative aunt, for she had done so at a house party once, and been kept awake half the night with her chatter. "It would be more comfortable to be together, and safer," she added, but with little relish.

"That was my thought. I took the larger room. It is at the far end of the hall, on the right. It's called the Three Cygnets, our room. Here, take the key and freshen yourself for dinner while I give them our order. We shan't change."

Vanessa went above, carefully watching room signs to discover which was theirs. The White Swan had suites called after its name: the Great Swan, La Plume and such things. At the end of the hall, she slid the bulky brass key into the lock, turned it, but the door did not open. She turned it back again, and the door opened instantly. Elleri had gone away and left it open, she thought with a little

spurt of annoyance. What if the letter had been there, in
her valise? Anyone might have walked off with it. But as
she entered, she saw their cases had not yet been brought
up. She worried why Harrow had not done so. Surely there
had been time. She took a step into the center of the room
to survey it, and was felled from a swift, hard blow to the
back of her head. She was immediately knocked unconscious, without even experiencing much pain. When she
opened her eyes a few moments later, she found herself
stretched out on the canopied bed, with her clothing all
disarranged.

"Oh, my God!" she exclaimed, sitting up and looking
all around her, frightened. Her assailant was gone. There
was a dull ache in her head, but she had already had a little
headache when she alit from the carriage, and did not fear
she had been permanently or seriously disabled. Looking
down, she saw the neck of her gown was open, her skirts
mussed. She felt certain she had been subjected to attack
by a sexual maniac of some sort. But he had hardly had
time to do more than *look*, she thought. She knew she had
not been violated, and though she was frightened half to
death, she was not in the state of hysteria the worse fate
would have caused.

The door was closed. Her next thought was to get out it,
down to her aunt and safety. She leapt from the bed,
fussing with her gown, then saw on the floor, at her feet,
her reticule, its contents shaken onto the floor, the straw
bag severed from its silken lining. She picked it up, stuffed
the contents hurriedly into it and ran along the corridor
quickly, feeling that every door was likely to send a
pursuer after her.

Her aunt was just issuing from a small room belowstairs,
and smiled at her. "You look a perfect fright, pet. Come
in and have a glass of wine. It will put some color back in
your cheeks. I have ordered . . ."

"Elleri, I have been attacked!" Vanessa said.

Without a word, her aunt grabbed her wrist and pulled
her into the private parlor. "Never say it in public, Nessie.
It would give people such an odd idea of your character.
Attacked, you say? The villain! We'll not stay another minute

in this place. We shall report it to the manager at once, and to the constable. . . . Only it is very vulgar. Oh, dear, and if they want you to be giving evidence, my dear, I would not *dream* of it. Word would be sure to get about you were raped. *Nothing* is more likely to ruin your reputation. You weren't, were you?''

"No, it is not that. Don't you see? Someone was after the letter.''

"Rubbish. Why would anyone want to read Henry's foolishness? He can't get Forrester to listen to a word he says. He is only complaining to Sir Giles of goings-on at the garrison. And how would anyone know we are here? Depend on it, the brute was planning to ravish you. He certainly had not time to do it; you were not gone above two minutes. Oh, what should we do? What would Henry want?''

"He would want us to make sure the letter is safe. Thank God I did not put it where Papa suggested, or it would certainly have been stolen. My reticule too was dismantled, my clothing searched—there can be no other explanation.''

"Was your money stolen? It might have been a simple robbery.''

Nessa scrambled amongst the rubble of lining and oddments in her reticule, to extract a leather money bag holding all her money.

"Mercy, I wonder if you could be right,'' Elleri said, turning a shade paler. "That was a shabby trick Henry played us, sending us into such danger. Why did he not send Parkins?''

"I have no idea, unless he required Parkins at home to help him in the affair. This is something more dangerous and excit—important than we thought, Auntie. Oh, the letter! I must get it from Harrow. Why didn't you lock our room door?''

"I *did* lock it. I remember perfectly well turning the key, and twisting the knob to see it was locked.''

"My valise was not in it, I hope?'' Vanessa asked, her eyes staring in horror.

"No, indeed. He had not brought the cases in yet. It

was only my traveling clock I took up. There is a clock
here on the wall, you see, so I left it abovestairs. I always
carry it into the inn myself, for it is quite valuable. They
did not used to have many clocks in inns in the old days,
for they were taxed most dreadfully, which is why Papa
bought mine.''

''I must get the letter. I shan't let it out of my sight
again.'' She ran into the lobby, to see Harrow just coming
with her own and her aunt's small cases. ''Your jewels are
all right and tight, ma'am,'' he said. ''I didn't let it out of
my sight. You'll be wanting the trunk left strapped on the
carriage, I fancy?''

''Yes, thank you, Harrow,'' she said. ''Just bring the
cases into our parlor, if you please.''

''Could I not take 'em up to your room for you?''

''No, we'll keep them with us.''

Miss Simons sat sipping wine and fanning herself with
her handkerchief, vexed to no small degree by all the
many unpleasant happenings of the day. ''The Fischers
would be sitting down to dinner now with Colonel Forrester
and half a dozen officers, and how are *we* to spend our
evening? Sitting in a very ugly inn room, looking at each
other.''

There was more of the same sort of talk, all of which
went unheeded as Vanessa unfastened her valise and lifted
her petticoats to extract the envelope, safe and sound where
she had put it. ''What shall I do with it?'' she asked.

''Put it into the mail,'' her aunt said angrily.

This too went unheeded. The bodice seemed a poor
spot, the first place the man had looked. The reticule was
no safer, yet she strongly wished to keep it about her own
person. Her light muslin gown boasted no pockets. In
desperation, she raised her skirts and stuck it down the top
of her stocking, where it felt as cumbersome as a stiff
sheet of cardboard, and as dangerous as a poison snake.
Then dinner arrived, and they sat down to eat.

Elleri chattered on about the raised pigeon pie, the sauce
quite good, but the crust as tough as tanned leather. And
where, one wondered, had they found such chewy peas, so
original. The syllabub was denigrated as certainly having

been made with old milk, when anyone knew it was only edible if rushed from cow to kitchen. Throughout the meal, Vanessa was minutely aware of the bulge in her stocking. While Elleri reverted, over coffee, to the Fischer dinner party, Vanessa began to wonder whether she should not have the carriage called out and continue the journey with a fresh team, not stopping at all till they had reached Sir Giles. Elleri, she knew, would balk at this uncomfortable plan, but she mentioned it anyway.

"You are a widgeon, Nessa. What would be easier than holding us up on a pitch-black road in the dead of night, with no one but Gretch and Harrow to come to our rescue? It is the most foolhardy thing you could possibly do. We shall bolt our door here, and take turns about staying up all night if you wish. I never sleep anyway; it will make no difference to me, I assure you."

These claims of insomnia were totally unfounded. Elleri often dozed off in front of the grate at home by nine o'clock in the evening. But going alone down an empty, dark highway *did* suggest more danger than Vanessa liked to consider, so she had half decided to remain overnight. This decision still wrinkled her brow when a tap was heard at the door.

"I never saw such a place," Elleri exclaimed, rolling up her eyes in disgust. "Servants knocking, requiring one to either get up and go to the door or holler like a fishwife. Leave it; we don't require anything. If they don't know enough to come in, let them go away."

The tap was repeated, more forcefully this time, with none of the timidity of a servant seeking entrance. Vanessa clutched at the top of her stocking. She knew in her bones it was someone after the letter.

CHAPTER
Five

"WE SHOULD HAVE locked the door!" she whispered to Miss Simons.

"You had better answer it, before they knock it down."

"Don't!" she said, holding on to the sides of her chair in an instinctive act.

Again the door was hit, even louder than before. Elleri got up, her face set in lines of disgruntlement, and strode forward, throwing the door open wide. Expecting no more than a waiter, she blinked to observe a swarthy, elegantly-dressed young gentleman. His hair was barbered closely, but she had become accustomed to this style from the officers around home. It was rather his dark skin and dark eyes that struck her attention.

He looked past her to Vanessa. "Miss Bradford?" he asked, in a deep voice.

The enquiry caused instant alarm. How should a total stranger know her name? Obviously he had been enquiring after her. She considered a denial, but already he was taking a long stride forward, into their private parlor, and still speaking. "I am Colonel Landon," he said. "I hope I have not frightened you. Your father sent me to help you.''

It seemed utterly unlikely her father was intimately acquainted with a colonel of such young years; his friends were older men. She knew as well he would not send a man who was *unknown* to him to help on this delicate mission. And if he were a colonel, as his hair suggested, why did he wear a civilian's blue jacket? She knew the local officers too, at least by sight. She had never seen this man before.

''Help me?'' she asked, parrying for time. ''I'm afraid I don't understand, sir.''

''With the letter,'' he said bluntly. ''He was worried about your going alone. Is it safe?''

''I don't know what you're talking about. You have made some mistake,'' she said, with a warning look to her aunt, who sat wild-eyed, fanning herself.

''You don't have to pretend with me,'' the man went on impatiently, even rudely. ''I am an officer, and a friend of your father.''

''Where did you meet him?'' Miss Bradford asked.

''At Levenhurst, this morning.''

''I mean previously, where did you make his acquaintance?''

''I didn't know him before, except by reputation. I was sent to the coast to overlook the preparations for defense there, not only in your own area, but all along the coast. I consider the Rye-Hastings area the most likely of attack. He told me what he discovered. Its importance is so great that we decided I should take the letter to London myself, and let you and your aunt return home.''

Vanessa could scarcely suppress a sneer at this blatant effort to seize her letter. London! He didn't even know where she was going, but only guessed at the likeliest destination. ''I have already told you, I have no letter,'' she repeated.

''I knew how it would be!'' he said, shaking his head. ''I told him he shouldn't have sent two ladies to deliver it.'' His expression was a blend of amusement and impatience. Looking around for a chair, he waited for Vanessa to sit down before he did so. He seemed perfectly at ease, which was more than could be said for the ladies. Vanessa was trembling inwardly, while Elleri was ready to go into a fit of vapors.

"It would be nice to be able to go home," the aunt suggested, with a timid, hopeful look.

"Your father feared he had given you so strong an idea of the letter's importance that you would not part with it, in which case he wished me to accompany you," the man said, in a very businesslike manner. "But I wish you would let *me* guard the letter. I would feel safer if I had it in my own care. You are perfectly welcome to come along to London." She noticed he again gave the wrong destination, but had of course no thought of correcting him. "A young lady—you might be hit on the head one of these dark nights as you walk along a quiet corridor, and have it stolen. I suppose you keep it on your person, as he asked? I would not like to think it sits unprotected in your room." He regarded her expectantly, waiting for confirmation of its hiding place.

"I am not likely to have on me a letter I know nothing of," she answered curtly. "My aunt and I are going to visit friends."

"Yes, yes, of course you are. I know all the instructions, Miss Bradford, and know they are mere subterfuge to fool the man who might be following you. Please, *trust* me. I should have had Colonel Bradford write a note introducing me and my mission. I wish we had thought of it, but it was all decided in a great rush, you know. Overtaking you seemed more important at the time than convincing you of my job. How should I know all your business if your father did not tell me?"

"You are singularly misinformed on my business, Colonel," she answered. "I cannot think of any reason anyone should hit me on the head some dark night, or bright afternoon, for that matter, can you?"

"I hardly think he'd strike in broad daylight," he answered, "but the *why* of it at least must be obvious, even to a woman."

"Yes, we ladies *do* have minds," she said quickly.

"Minds of your own! The whole area along the east coast is alive with spies. Your father feared, and I agree with him, that your trip might cause suspicion. No less than three callers had been to ask for you before I arrived."

"Was Colonel Forrester one of them?" Miss Simons asked eagerly.

"No, they were all ladies, I believe. They expressed a great astonishment you should have deserted home on the day of some ball. Your father's active involvement with the volunteers is well known. His position as a retired colonel subjects him and his family to a close scrutiny by the French element."

Nessa noticed at this point that her caller was setting aside a newspaper he had held in his hand when he entered. He had shapely, strong hands, well able to knock a girl unconscious and search her. She blushed suddenly, to think what familiarity this stranger had taken with her. And he was examining her closely now too, her whole body. "Where have you got it?" he asked bluntly. "Don't waste precious time denying its existence. I didn't come all this way to play games." His manner was changing from impatience to bold arrogance, with even something of menace.

She did not bother to repeat knowing nothing of the letter, but only thought how to be rid of him as quickly as possible. "My aunt and myself have had a very tiring day. We plan to go to bed now. Good evening, sir." She walked to the door and held it, with a commanding stare at the man.

"We can't leave it like this! I must know it is safe. I wish you will let me have it."

"You may rest assured any charge my father placed on me will be executed. Good evening."

"Wait!"

"If you do not leave us this instant, I shall call the manager."

"We don't want any ruckus. I'll go along with you for protection, if you don't want me to carry it. We must arrange our plans for the morning. At what hour did you plan to leave?"

"My father failed to tell you that, did he?" she asked satirically. There was some traffic in the hall, lending her a sense of security.

"He said early. In the Army, if you are not aware of it, *early* is not ten o'clock, but the crack of dawn. Give me your room's designation, and I shall undertake to keep an eye on your door through the night. I don't have to tell you to lock the door, and make some precaution at the window as well."

"No, and you don't have to tell us to dry behind our ears either. I doubt a locked door would keep out such a dangerous spy as *you* speak of."

"I'm glad you realize it. The letter must *never* be left untended, with only a lock to protect it. I could open any locked door in this establishment with my clasp knife."

"Are you a pick-lock as well as a colonel?"

"At times. Am I to understand the letter *is* on your person?" he asked boldly. Again his eyes roved over her gown, selecting possible places of concealment as they lingered on her bodice. She could not prevent a blush of embarrassment, but it was anger that lent a fiery hue to her eyes. She glared, silent.

"We have not chosen our hour for departure," he went on calmly. "Six should be early enough to beat the crowds, and it will give us a few hours' rest. I don't bèlieve you gave me your room."

"I don't believe I did," she answered, then tried to push his resisting form out the door. He planted his feet apart and stood solid.

"I must say I did not expect *this* treatment! You are going to have my protection, whether you want it or no, and when you return home, I shall expect an apology, Miss Bradford. Ladies." He executed a bow and strolled off at a leisurely gait, without bothering to look back when the door slammed.

"I never saw such gall!" Miss Bradford exclaimed.

"Shocking. But if he was telling the truth, Nessa, it would be nice to be rid of that pesty letter, would it not? We could go to London instead of Ipswich, and do some shopping."

"He didn't even know our destination. He was not sent from Papa. That is the man who attacked me in our room. Having failed by direct means, he has invented this ruse."

"Could we not slip the letter into the post?"

"Papa trusted me to do this job, and I come to realize now how important it is. He's probably listening at the door. Let us go to our room to discuss it. We'll take the valises up ourselves."

Elleri heaved herself up from the chair, picking up the discarded newspaper to read in her room before sleeping. Together they went into the hallway. The man who called himself Colonel Landon was at the desk, in conversation with the clerk. He turned to speak to them as they passed. "I shall be keeping an eye on the Three Cygnets," he said in a low tone. A triumphant glitter sparkled in his eyes.

Vanessa's bosom swelled with indignation, but she said not a word till they were beyond his hearing. They entered their chamber, locked the door and checked to see the window was bolted. "Auntie, we must leave here this very night, at once," Vanessa said.

"I doubt I'll be able to make it to the bed, much less the carriage. Every bone and joint in my poor body aches. Gretch rattled us along at a merciless pace, no matter how often I pulled the check string. It is all Henry's doings. And where should we go? He would only follow us to another inn. I *do* think we should post the letter."

"There is no post leaving at this hour of the night. If we left it here, it would sit unprotected in some box where anyone might pick it up. Papa would have mailed it if he trusted the post. There are often robberies from the mail coach. No, we shall deliver the letter in person, but to succeed, we must be rid of Landon. At least he does not know our destination."

"He'll soon know it's not London we're headed to, when we pass by it, won't he?"

"All the more reason to leave at once."

"I was looking forward to a quiet read of this paper I picked up downstairs," she said, looking down at it. "Bother, it is all in French. After studying it for ten years, I still cannot make heads or tails of it."

"French!" Vanessa squealed. "Where did you get that?"

"That fellow left it in our parlor. Oh, my goodness!" she gasped, sinking down onto a chair. "Nessie, you are right! Colonel Landon is a French spy! Imagine, they have infiltrated our army."

"He's no more a colonel than I am. Colonel Landon indeed! Monsieur Ladonnée is more like it."

"I confess I thought you were making a mountain of a mole hill, as young girls will always do. The fellow was casting such sheep's eyes on you, I thought he was only trying to scrape an acquaintance, but it begins to seem . . ."

"Wolf's eyes is more like it. He was positively *frightening*. Certainly he is a spy." The French paper confirmed in her mind that her attacker was Landon. It also inclined Miss Simons to see the advantages of an immediate remove from the White Swan. The next decision was where to go instead. Any inn would be equally precarious. Their carriage's leaving the stable would be reported to the spy, and he would be after them.

"Do we know anyone close by we could go to? He could not follow us to a private home if we got away before he saw us. What we must do is take our cases downstairs on tiptoe, and have Gretch bring the carriage around as quickly as possible. We'll be safe standing in the lobby."

"The only soul I know within ten miles is the Raffertys, and I would prefer being assaulted to going near them," Miss Simons said, her face falling in chagrin. "We would do better to dart to London—the Halfords or Staceys . . ."

"No, he *thinks* we are going to London. That is the direction he will take. What is amiss with these Raffertys?"

"They are *Methodists*, my dear. We would have a perfectly wretched time. They do not believe in drink, or music or any of the refinements of life. Mrs. Rafferty was a Featherstone before her marriage, and a friend of mine years ago. But she married a Methodist, and there is no doing anything for her now. I made the wretched error of stopping there once on my way from London to Levenhurst, and vowed I would never darken her door again."

"You will darken it tonight, Auntie, and so will I. It is not refinement we are after, but safety. How far away is it?"

"I remember there were lime trees in the orchard," Elleri stated unhelpfully.

"Yes, but where was the house?"

"It cannot be far from Tilbury. The *highlight* of our visit was a dart into this pokey place to look at a church, in the rain. About three miles away, I think, but I cannot recall in which direction precisely."

"Ring the bell. We'll send a servant to the stable to have our carriage readied and brought around before the colonel gets to our keyhole. Can't you remember the direction? *Try.*"

"I've got it now! It is north, the right direction for us. We *weren't* coming from London but from Cambridge, when Jane's son was . . . ."

"Good," Vanessa said, to interrupt the tale before it began. "Now let us invent an excuse for barging in on the Raffertys at such a farouche hour."

"We'll be lucky if they're not in bed with the doors locked. There can be *no* excuse for rousing folks up out of their beds at night. Really, it would not be at all the thing, dear."

"Sickness is always an excuse for doing the inexcusable."

"That is true, and it would give me an *excellent* excuse not to have to sit down and talk to them. I shall say we were going to Cambridge, but developed a sick stomach from Gretch's cow-handling of the ribbons. Excellent! There will be no need for you to stay chatting more than half an hour. Claim fatigue and join me. Now all we require is an excuse for going to Cambridge. Jane's son is no longer there."

"It doesn't have to be Cambridge. We'll say London was our goal."

"But we would not have gone to London via Tilbury, my dear. They are foolish, but not at all stupid. They know their map as well as anyone."

This reminded Vanessa that Landon had certainly followed them by sight, for had he been told London was their destination, he would not have been on the right road. It was odd he had made such an obvious blunder, when she considered it a moment longer.

They took up their cases, slipped silently along the corridor to the stairs and made it to the clerk's desk without seeing their spy. While Vanessa looked out for the carriage, Elleri went to the desk to settle their reckoning and try her hand at getting a lower rate owing to their early departure. She thought it grossly unfair to pay a whole night's lodging when they had not even mussed the bed, but was too anxious to spend long arguing.

"Would you happen to know how to get to John Rafferty's place?" she asked, as an afterthought. "It is called Oakdene—an old stone place three or so miles away."

The clerk was familiar with it, and gave her exact instructions to reach it. She was able to tell Gretch how to get there, which surprised Vanessa, pleasantly so. She did not question it, however. It did not so much as cross her mind her aunt had left word behind where they were headed.

"I think Papa would be proud of how well we are managing matters," she said with satisfaction. "I had not realized I had a flare for deception, till I tried it."

"Women are born with a knack for deception," she was told. "How else should they ever get husbands to marry them? There is a deal of deception in nabbing a parti. Take Miss Fischer, now, letting on her hair is naturally curly, and her sly mama, inviting Forrester to dinner."

Vanessa hardly listened to this topic that would normally engage her full attention. She felt through her skirt to see the letter was still resting in the top of her stocking, then sat back to devise excuses for landing in on the Raffertys so late at night.

CHAPTER
Six

*I*T WAS NOT at all a long drive to Raffertys. Though the road was dark and lonesome, causing much concern for highwaymen or spies who acted as such, they arrived in safety at the front door of a moldering stone mansion that looked large enough to house them without inconvenience. They were greeted by a disapproving butler, much put out to have to announce callers at nine-thirty in the evening. The lady of the house was equally displeased to have to make them welcome.

It was hard to credit this lean-cheeked woman with thin gray hair pulled severely back from her forehead was of an equal age with Aunt Elleri. Her gaunt frame was covered in a very plain gray gown, unadorned by so much as a collar, or inch of lace. Her spouse was equally austere. They had been sitting in state, the two of them, in a pair of wing chairs before a cold grate, with no cards, no books or magazines and no conversation.

The feeble excuse for stopping was put forth, causing some confusion when Elleri mentioned Cambridge as their destination and Vanessa simultaneously said Colchester. A sort of tepid welcome was proferred, soon followed by equally tepid tea. After one small cup, Miss Simons sighed and explained her head would split wide open if she did not place it on a pillow at once. Vanessa was left alone with two aging strangers, who were not adept at small talk.

There was really only one subject of conversation in any house at this time. The name of Napoleon soon arose, allowing a brief respite from the silence while Miss Bradford related what facts she remembered having heard her father mention. "Who is in charge there, anyway?" Mr. Rafferty demanded.

"Colonel Forrester," she answered, with a wrench to consider that now the ball would be getting into full swing. The orange trees would be giving off their perfume, the silk sheets making an intimate roof over the heads of Miss Fischer and Miss Condie and all the fortunate ladies who were standing up with the commandant, but of course the heinous word "ball" did not intrude into this Methodist sanctuary.

Mrs. Rafferty said she disapproved of all Frenchmen on principle, and Mr. Rafferty pronounced that Napoleon ought to be drawn and quartered if he dared to set a toe on England, and so he would be, by Jehosephat. Miss Bradford taxed her ingenuity to think of another subject to pass the next half hour, at which time she felt she could decently retire. She jumped six inches from her chair when the front-door knocker pounded.

"Who the deuce can be calling at such an hour?" Mr. Rafferty snorted with an accusing look at his wife. "Bad enough people we scarcely know . . ." His eyes just peeled off the top of Vanessa's head, to intercept a repressive stare from his wife, who was not quite such a savage as her husband.

"Why don't you go and see?" she asked pretty sharply. He arose, but before he reached the doorway, there was the sound of a young gentleman's voice asking for Mr. Edward Rafferty. The lady of the house addressed her husband as John, so Vanessa assumed there was a son on the premises, one with the wits to have removed himself from the saloon.

"Edward is not at home," Mrs. Rafferty said. "Who can be calling on him?"

The butler marched to the archway to announce in injured accents, "Mr. Carlisle."

A well-formed young man entered, elegantly got up in dark clothing. He smiled politely. He was not exactly handsome, but he had a winning smile and rather happy eyes—blue eyes. Had he been only a quarter as presentable, he would have been a welcome addition to the party, in the lady's view. He bowed politely to the ladies before giving Mr. Rafferty's hand a shake.

"I understand your son is away?" he asked, looking surprised to hear it.

"He is gone off to some races," the mother told him, with deep disapproval.

"He must have gone to the Doncaster meet. Odd he did not mention it," Carlisle replied, apparently not realizing that racing, tinged as it was with gambling, was a taboo in this household.

"Very likely," the dame agreed. "Did you wish to see Edward?"

"We had an appointment," Mr. Carlise said. "He invited me to visit him two weeks ago, to come on this date. We were to go to London together. Odd he did not let me know he was leaving."

"Well, he is not here," Mrs. Rafferty repeated, just casting her eyes about the room as though to hint he could see for himself.

Miss Bradford was made acquainted with him, which brought him to a chair beside her. "Visiting, are you?" he asked pleasantly.

"Miss Bradford is staying overnight with us," the Hostess explained. "Would you care for a cup of tea before you leave, Mr. Carlisle?"

"Leave?" he asked, his brows rising. "But surely Edward will be here tomorrow morning. We had a definite appointment."

"Oh, you want to stay overnight," Rafferty said in an accusing way.

"I would not want to put you to any trouble," he said quickly, even apologetically. "I can go to an inn, if there is one nearby."

An inn was likely to serve him strong drink, a thing to be avoided at whatever personal inconvenience to the Raffertys, as the man was a friend of their son. "It will be no trouble," the woman said, her thin voice belying the generous words.

"You are very kind," he said, accepting a cup of tea.

The parents' hostility thawed somewhat over the tea. "So you are a friend of Edward's, are you?" Mr. Rafferty confirmed. "A friend from his university days, I daresay. He met all manner of riffraff there."

"Just so," Mr. Carlisle replied gravely, but with some laughter lurking in those blue eyes.

"Are you the fellow who lives at Birmingham?" Rafferty continued, in an accusing way, his brows gathering in dismay. Miss Bradford thought that if she were the visitor, she would not admit to ever having been near Birmingham. "Edward went to a ball in Birmingham."

"Oh, really?" Carlisle asked, quite obviously nonplussed by this piece of information. "No, I am from the Cotswold Hills."

"Yes, I think I have you placed now," Rafferty said wisely. "Edward goes there every year for the hunting. I daresay it is *you* he visits."

"He has visited me at home twice," Carlisle admitted.

Nessa could see plainly he was uneasy with this pair of Tartars. She took the idea he would be much more amusing on his own than in this company. He turned to her and made a few polite enquiries as to her place of origin, then expressed some familiarity with the area. Again the subject of Napoleon's possible invasion came up, to occupy a few minutes. When it got at last to be ten o'clock, Nessa glanced at the long-case clock standing against the wall, wondering if she could politely express her fatigue.

"Time for your medicine, John," Mrs. Rafferty said, rising up like a puppet at the first gong from the clock.

One had the idea their whole life was similarly regulated by clocks. A servant appeared promptly at the doorway, without having to be summoned. He bore a tray of bottles and droppers, giving the impression Rafferty was a professional invalid. "Will you excuse us?" Mrs. Rafferty said. "I have to measure John's medications." She went nearer the lamp to do so.

Carlisle once again turned to Miss Bradford. "Lively evening," he said with a playful smile. The married couple spoke between themselves, allowing some privacy to the others.

"Livelier than they are accustomed to or can quite like, I think," Vanessa answered with a deprecating smile of her own. "My arrival too was unexpected."

"You escape tomorrow morning, if I understood correctly?" he asked.

"As soon as the cock crows, I promise you."

"I shall do likewise if Edward does not come. He's a devilish-odd chap, Edward. Do you know him?"

"No, I am a stranger here, which makes my welcome not entirely enthusiastic. It is my aunt who is a friend, but she has gone to bed with a headache."

"She is wise. It would be her previous acquaintance that accounts for the headache. I wonder what can account for her stopping at all?"

His whole tone was facetious. As there was no fear he was after her letter, she answered, "It was a dire emergency, sir."

"On your way home, are you?"

"No, I have just come from home. We are going to visit friends at Ipswich."

"Ipswich? I don't believe I know anyone there."

"Family friends," she said, seeing no reason to mention a name.

"Edward and I have planned a week of partying in the city. He often speaks of his parents as being strict, but I had no idea they were so gothic, till I stumbled in tonight. I shall leave at the crack of dawn if he is not here tonight."

"Don't you think you should give him till mid-morning?" she asked.

"I imagine he has forgotten all about my visit. Actually, I was supposed to arrive at noon today myself, but got held up. If he is *still* not here, you know, it is unlikely he is coming at all. But I do not give up hope of him yet. He may arrive before we are sent off to bed. Do you suppose that battalion of bottles is to prepare Mr. Rafferty for a peaceful night? I doubt we'll be allowed to remain in the saloon without his chaperonage."

"I was just calculating what hour would be not *too* uncivil to retire," she answered.

"I begin to wonder if I would not be wiser to go to an inn. Do you happen to know if there is one close by?"

"There is an inn at Tilbury—the White Swan. I noticed it as we came by," she told him.

"Probably full at this hour."

She did not contradict him, though she doubted her own lately abandoned room was taken yet.

There was a positive snort from the corner when the door knocker was sounded for a *third* time. "Bad news always comes in threes," Mr. Rafferty said fatalistically, while Nessa held back a smile by biting her lip, and Carlisle laughed softly. "I own *I* am little enough addition to the party, but I think he is hard to call *you* bad news, ma'am," he consoled her. Really he had the nicest smile, so open and confiding, yet with some intimacy too. It was the way he worked his eyes that did it, looking deeply into hers. Even Forrester had not such a winning smile.

Another masculine voice sounded in the hallway, the tones of it familiar to Vanessa, who inhaled sharply. Her hand flew to her mouth in an instinctive gesture of shocked dismay.

"What is it?" Carlisle asked, leaning forward quickly to look at her more closely.

"It's Colonel Landon! Oh, dear—I . . ." She looked about the room, seeking, in her befuddled state, a place to hide.

Within seconds, Colonel Landon stood framed in the doorway, while the butler announced, "Mr. Kiley," in a state of exasperation which he made no effort to conceal.

"I *do* beg your pardon, sir," Landon said, walking

forward, toward Rafferty. "I have had the worst piece of luck. I broke an axle, just on the road outside of your place, and have come to ask directions to the nearest stable." Even as he spoke, his eyes flickered to Vanessa, leveling an accusing glare on her.

She looked back, as though she had seen a ghost. "Who is he? Is something the matter, Miss Bradford?" Carlisle asked her.

"I don't know who he is. Oh, dear, what am I to do?"

"Has he been bothering you? Is he following you?"

She was unsure how much she should tell him, but began to look at Carlisle with a new interest. If Edward did not come, Mr. Carlisle was at loose ends and might help her out of her difficulty.

"Come, now, tell me the truth," Carlisle urged with an encouraging look.

"I can't tell you. Not now—not here."

The conversation at the medications table was meanwhile going forth apace. Mr. Rafferty took delight in the broken axle, and the reason for it was not long kept to himself. "I've told them a dozen times that road wants fixing. Holes so big you could get lost in them. *I* broke an axle two weeks ago. I only save my carriage by driving along the edge, with one wheel half in the ditch. A stranger at night—it was bound to happen. Maybe *now* they'll tend to it. You want to report it in town, sir."

"I certainly will," Landon answered with good humor. "My problem at the moment is how to get into town."

"There won't be anyone at the municipal office at this hour. Go tomorrow morning."

"Yes, but where shall I stable my team and myself tonight?"

"You might as well stay here. Everyone else is. No one will come from the stables for you at this hour of the night. No one is willing to put himself out, even to make money. The world is going to ruin."

"It is the drink that causes it," Landon said after taking careful note of the teacups scattered about the room.

"You've hit it right on the head, lad! And where does

the drink come from? From *France*, that is where. The wine, at least. It is Bonaparte who is at the bottom of it."

"You're absolutely right," Landon said firmly.

Nessa knew she was not imagining the fleeting smile of triumph that flickered over Landon's face. When he cast a swift look at her, her heart sank. He went into the hall with Mr. Rafferty. Before long—not more than ten minutes had passed—they were back. He had actually worked Rafferty up to a smile. She listened with keen interest to learn how he had worked this miracle. Even his wife was staring in disbelief.

It was the war they were discussing, expressing every revulsion with Bonaparte, but Landon made no claims to being a soldier. What he appeared to have become was a government inspector of supplies for the Army. He had gauged his host's temper, and was inveighing against corruption in the business—shoddy goods delivered at inflated prices. The world was not only going to ruin, but gone. There wasn't an honest man between Land's End and Dover, with the exception of themselves.

"Even my own son—I hate to admit it—takes his bottle of wine a day," Rafferty said, the smile fast fading at this profligacy.

"Three is more like it," Carlisle said in a low voice.

Mrs. Rafferty belonged to that numerous company of ladies who take their views from their husbands. When she saw John approved of Mr. Kiley, she sent off for a fresh pot of tea. After it was brought in, the two earlier guests were invited to join the other circle around the cold grate. Mr. Kiley was presented to them. He put on a polite face and said to Vanessa, "How do you do? I believe I am acquainted with your father, ma'am. Colonel Bradford, is it not?"

"Yes," she said sharply, and added not another word. As the tea was slowly drunk, Carlisle joined the conversation. The hosts were more sociable now, perhaps because the third and last nuisance had been visited upon them. It gave Kiley a moment to speak to Vanessa.

"That was an ill-advised move on your part, bolting from the inn," he told her.

"How did you know? Did you follow me?"

"Not immediately. I don't mind traveling on an empty stomach, but after twelve hours' fast, a man must eat something. As your aunt was kind enough to leave directions to her destination at the desk, there was no difficulty in finding you."

"She didn't! Oh, the foolish . . ."

"Folly on both your parts. Don't be too hasty in sloughing off the blame. I have discovered by now which of you is in command of the operation. Where is the letter? Does your aunt have it abovestairs?"

She lifted her chin and glared at him, without answering. He continued on, oblivious to her snubs. "Don't leave it with her. She is even more shatter-brained than yourself. Leaving your direction at the inn, my God! Anyone would have easy work of the pair of you. Have you got it on you now?" She could never become accustomed to those bold, dark eyes, examining her anatomy with the closest scrutiny. She remained rigidly silent, but he spoke on, with an occasional glance toward the other group, as though he were half listening to it. "Actually, coming here was not a bad idea, had you told me first and brought me along."

"We only came to get away from *you*."

"That gives me some idea of the high regard in which I am held. Did you not know any friendly undertakers or tooth drawers you might have gone to instead? How on earth do you come to be acquainted with such gothic characters?"

"One has, unfortunately, not always a choice in one's acquaintances," she said.

"Touché. Was the callow Carlisle also foisted on you against your will? Who is he? Was he here when you arrived?"

"No, he was not, and I don't know who he is."

"How long after you came did he show up?"

"Half an hour, more or less. Why do you ask?"

"That makes the time about right. What excuse did he give for coming?"

"He is a friend of the family; he is *not* a French spy, and don't bother hinting that he is."

"Not all who spy for France are of French origin."

"I know that! Neither do they all read French newspapers. Only the more careless amongst them leave such obvious clues."

"I left it behind, did I? I was wondering where I had dropped it. I hold *you* to blame." She looked up questioningly at this speech. "Yes, your father told me only that you were a vain, silly girl, you see. He did not mention what good reason you have for your vanity. I did not picture you a fragile blonde at all. You must favor your mama in appearance, as well as—er, character?" he said, with a quizzing smile.

"I am not *silly* enough to overlook the French newspaper in any case," she answered curtly. "And if my father thought so, he would not have sent me . . ." She came to an angry silence, while a sly smile spread over Landon's harsh features.

"Certainly he would not have given you the letter had he thought so. At last you admit that he *did*."

"I did not!"

"If it is the French paper that troubles you, let me explain. It is hardly incriminating, you know. We are all interested to discover what stories Boney is propagating to the common folks back in France. I personally pick one up whenever I can find it. If I were a French spy, I would not be caught dead with one. But enough of polite conversation. Let us get to bed before more of that dreadful, weak tea is foisted on us. We shall want an early start in the morning."

"*You—are—not—coming—with us,*" she said, weighting every word with heavy emphasis.

"How much do you want to wager?" he asked in a light tone. It was not hard to imagine even that he was laughing at her.

"Why did you change your name and pretend not to know me, if you are innocent?" she demanded.

He shrugged his shoulders. "It seemed a good idea at the time. Your father thought it a wise precaution that I change into mufti to detract attention from myself. The scarlet tunics are a trifle garish, you must own. As I was wearing civvies, I claimed a new job and name to go with them. Kiley struck me as having a good Methodist ring to it. I wish you had run to someone other than a Methodist. A glass of wine would go well before retiring.''

"I was not running *to* anyone, but *from* a gentleman even less amusing than Rafferty.''

"I can be tolerably amusing, under the proper conditions. There is not the least need for this journey to be so unpleasant. *I* have outgrown my love of hare and hounds quite a few years ago. In fact, as I *did* accidentally crack the axle of my carriage in that demmed hole in the road, I shall have to join you and your aunt in yours instead. We shall leave at seven. It is difficult to get out of a polite household earlier, or even an impolite one, such as this,'' he added with a considering look around him. "Be ready,'' he told her.

It was a command, no less. She took a deep breath, ready to tell him her feelings in the matter. He lifted a hand and out-talked her. "Miss Bradford, pray do not make it necessary for me to steal Mr. Carlisle's carriage and undertake any more journeys this night. *You* had the advantage of sitting at ease in your carriage; *I* have been driving all day.''

"We were not *at ease,* but bounced around mercilessly!''

"Poor child. Is *that* what has put you in such an almighty pucker? One really feels for the sufferings that are endured on the home front—the higher taxes, the occasional shortage of silk or brandy. Sometimes I feel we soldiers have the better of the bargain, only having to dodge bullets and occasionally go without food or bed. But I shall shed a tear for you another time. Having the luxury of a bed awaiting me tonight, I would like to get a few hours' use from it. I would sleep better if you would tell me where you have put the letter.''

"You can quit staring at my—*me,* sir. You must know by now I do not carry it on me. You didn't find it when you searched me, did you?''

He set his cup down with a clatter. "What?" he asked, in a voice loud enough to draw attention from the corner.

"What's that you say, Mr. Kiley?" Mrs. Rafferty asked.

"Miss Bradford was just speaking of some doings at the garrison at Hastings," he improvised smoothly. "It appears there is a ball going forth this minute."

"That's how they waste our money," Rafferty said, delighted to launch into another tirade. "There'll be drinking and dancing and carousing."

"You were wise to leave," Mrs. Rafferty told Vanessa. "You would not want to get mixed up with *officers*."

"I am trying my best to avoid it," she replied, with an innocent stare at Landon.

"Your own father is a colonel!" Rafferty reminded her.

"Retired," Landon mentioned in an exculpating way.

She could take no more. She arose and said her good evenings to the party. She directed a pleading look in Carlisle's direction, trying to signify she wished private words with him. He inclined his head slightly to tell her he understood. From the crevice of his eye, Landon observed the silent exchange, and was obliged to stifle the lively curse that rose to his lips.

Vanessa found her aunt, the insomniac, sleeping soundly, with light snores issuing from her open lips. She remained fully dressed till she heard the others mount the stairs to go to their rooms. With her ear to the closed door, she smiled with relief to hear Rafferty and Landon (or possibly Kiley) proceed well past her room, down toward the end of the hallway.

"Shocking bad manners, and her father a colonel," were the last words she could make out. It was Mr. Rafferty who spoke. Landon's reply was indistinguishable, but the tone was supportive.

CHAPTER
Seven

$\mathcal{M}$R. KILEY WAS not the only one who wanted a few hours of sleep. Vanessa too found it very hard to keep her eyes open, as she sat yawning, watching her candle grow shorter and wondering at what hour she could expect Mr. Carlisle to come to her. She was still in her dress, not wanting to allow him into her chamber at all, but determined to lend any propriety she could to the affair. At last he came. There was a gentle tap at the door. Carlisle had also remained fully dressed. She opened the door a crack to determine that it was indeed Carlisle, and not Mr. Kiley come to harangue her again.

"Shall we slip down to the saloon to talk?" he whispered. What a civil, gentlemanly suggestion. Had it been Kiley, he would have had his toe in the door and forced his way in. His commanding manner angered her greatly. *Be ready!* How dare he? She opened the door wider to go with him, along the dark hallway, down the stairs into the saloon.

"We'll risk one light," he said, groping in the dark for the tinder box.

While he did this, she considered exactly what she should tell him, for as she now realized the importance of what she carried, she did not plan to reveal the secret to anyone. She would invent some other ruse to gain his escort. He sat beside her on the sofa at a decent distance, obviously planning to behave himself. "Miss Bradford, I can see you are in some sort of a muddle, and assume it involves Mr. Kiley. Is he harassing you with his attentions?"

This sounded plausible, but hardly of sufficient import to request his company to Ipswich, when she had her aunt along as chaperone. "It is not a matter of romance," she said, turning to regard him closely in the poorly lit room. Really he had a very kind, open face. There was a strong urge to tell all, but she desisted. The thing was, he looked *too* kind, too innocent to handle Kiley. Still, he was the only likely candidate for the job. "No, the fact is, I carry with me an item of some considerable value which I believe he means to steal from me."

"I see," he nodded. "Jewelry or money?"

"Jewelry," she answered at once, as it sounded smaller than a box of gold. "A diamond necklace, belonging to my late mama. I am taking it . . ." Oh, dear! Where could one sensibly be taking a valuable diamond necklace? ". . . to have a copy made," she said, desperate for some reason, "in Ipswich."

"In *Ipswich?*" he asked with a little frown. Not disbelieving quite, but obviously thinking it a foolish arrangement for a young lady to be jaunting about the countryside carrying such a valuable item.

"The copy will be made in London, actually, but the friends I am visiting will arrange that. Papa decided to have it done while I was visiting close to London, you see."

"But Ipswich is as far from London as Hastings is," he pointed out.

"It will be done on my way home," she improvised quickly.

"I see. You have got it stored in a safe place?"

"Yes. Yes, I have, but Kiley is a desperate man. He would do anything to get it. He—he has made one attempt already. I cannot imagine how he discovered I am carrying it.''

"He mentioned knowing your family. Probably bribed a servant at your home.''

"Very likely,'' she agreed, thankful for his help in her fabrication.

"Why do you not report him to a constable?'' he asked. "You said he had made an attempt on it . . .''

"She floundered helplessly. "I—I cannot *prove* it, you see. There is no evidence, but I *know* it was he who made the attempt.''

"If you are quite certain about the danger, then I shall accompany you to Ipswich,'' he offered gallantly. "It is not likely Edward will come at all, and even if he does, we had planned on no more than amusing ourselves. I am at your disposal entirely, Miss Bradford. Only tell me in what way I can be of help.''

"Oh, thank you. You are so very kind. I hardly dared to ask you. It is a great imposition, I know.''

"Nonsense. I am delighted to be of service to a lady in distress. We men dream of such opportunities, but they too seldom arise. In what way can I help? Do you want me to deliver it for you? No, you would hardly care to entrust anything so valuable to a total stranger.''

"You are not a *total* stranger. A friend of the Raffertys, like myself.''

"Only to Edward, and as to that, you are practically a stranger to the family yourself.''

"I'm sure even a stranger to them must realize their *morals* are unquestionable.''

"Very true. I wonder if morality must be so heavy a burden as they make it. But we digress. Let us think what to do about your necklace. I think the thing to do is for me to accompany you. I shall follow immediately behind your carriage in my curricle, and we shall arrange to stop at the same places for meals and so on. Of course your groom will have taken some precautions as well?''

"Yes, indeed. Papa gave him a pistol, which is under the box, and a footman is along too. It is not the open road I fear so much as the stops, when I must be separated from

Gretch and Harrow. If we had a man to protect us during the stops, it would be very reassuring.''

''Well, then, you have one,'' he said, smiling.

It was exactly what she had hoped for. He was alive to every sense of propriety, not trying to get her valuable property away from her, not putting himself forward in the least, but just being there, to help if necessary. His kind face took on a stronger coloring of amiability in her view. ''We must leave early,'' she suggested next. ''Very early. I wonder at what hour it would be feasible to leave. Kiley mentioned seven. Do you think—would you mind terribly to be up at six, and leave as soon as we can? Rafferty will not try to detain us. I have the most sinking sensation we are not half welcome at Oakdene.''

''Is that what the place is called? We'll go any hour that suits you. I doubt Kiley will be up so early as six.''

Vanessa had a strong feeling he would be, but could hardly suggest darting out of the house in the middle of the night. She remembered with considerable pleasure that Kiley had a cracked axle to contend with, which would delay his departure considerably.

''Tell me, or am I imagining things—did you call Kiley by some other name when he came in?'' Carlisle asked.

''He uses various names and occupations. Colonel Landon is the name I know him by.''

''A man who requires an alias must be a blackguard. How did you meet up with such a bounder?''

''That is a long story, Mr. Carlisle, and I am sure you must be as fagged as I am myself. I'll tell you tomorrow. We had best go now, before we are discovered by our hostess, who would put the most licentious construction on our visit. We colonels' daughters rate one rung lower than an actress, I believe, in her code.''

''Prudes *do* tend to overestimate the world's wickedness, do they not?'' he commented, arising and offering his hand to help her up.

''I don't know how to thank you.''

''We shall strike on a reward when we discover how hard Mr. Kiley is to handle,'' he answered lightly. They blew out their light, to go in total darkness upstairs to their rooms. He left her at her door, then proceeded stealthily to his own room. Her heart was lighter as she turned the knob. A narrow shaft of faint light made her wonder whether she had left a candle burning behind her. She saw one on her dresser, and frowned at it, trying to remember, as she closed and bolted the door.

As she turned to face the bed, she emitted a faint shriek. There, holding her nightgown in his fingers, admiring the cascade of rippling lace, stood Mr. Kiley, wearing a bemused smile. "Very nice, Miss Bradford," he complimented, looking across the room at her.

"What are you doing here?"

"Hush! What will the Raffertys think of your behavior? Bad enough you had a tryst with Carlisle, without seducing an innocent government official into the bargain. I hope it was only a spot of romance that took you to the saloon?" he asked.

"Get out."

"I am very much disillusioned by your conduct, I can tell you," he went on calmly, leaning in a casual way against the bedpost. "Your papa *did* mention an inclination to flirt with the officers, but never suspected such unladylike goings-on as clandestine meetings. Don't blush, dear girl. You were unwittingly chaperoned the whole time, from behind the curtain, by that blackguard who requires a roster of aliases—me. I observed no letter changed hands, so assume it is safely stowed away. I am relieved to see you were not stupid enough to stick it beneath your pillow, or only slightly less stupidly, under the sheet or mattress. It is not in with your undergarments . . ."

"You had the audacity to rummage through my personal belongings!"

"I blame Kiley for it. Landon would not be so low. You *did* say you don't keep it on you, and all those hateful eye examinations tend to confirm it, unless it is a *very small* letter. Of more importance is for me to hear about this person who searched you. It was not I, which leads us to the overwhelming question—who was it? Somebody knows you have it, and that makes its delivery precarious. I want to hear all about that search."

"Search your memory. You have searched everything else!"

He ignored the remark. "It happened at the White Swan, I take it?"

She inclined her head slightly in agreement. "In your room. You certainly weren't there long. Did it happen before or after I met you in the parlor?"

"Before, the instant I entered the room, in fact."

"So he's followed you from Hastings, must have been on your tail all day. Did you notice anyone following you?"

"No, not anyone, including you."

"I wasn't close enough to be seen—several miles behind, as I got a late start. We'll have to check at the inn before we go, and see if we can discover who stopped shortly after you. The stables will be our best bet."

He sauntered slowly toward her door. "Don't forget to lock up tight behind me. I didn't even have to jimmy the lock, which hints at your carrying the letter somewhere under that delightful gown. Where *can* it be, I wonder?" he asked in a musing way, as though speaking to himself, but his eyes were riveted on her thighs. He even knew the spot where she had concealed it. "Must be fairly uncomfortable, I should think. I hope you have it well tucked in."

He left, without bothering to say good night. The bolt was slid to with a loud bang, but not loud enough to vent the half of her wrath. Entering her bedroom and searching her belongings, without so much as an apology! Upon my word, he had the gall for anything. No doubt he would have searched *her* again as well, had it not been for the Raffertys and Carlisle in the nearby rooms. It was all that had saved her. Those bold, dark eyes and tanned fingers sent a shiver up her spine. She next considered where to hide the letter for the night. Not under the pillow or sheet or mattress. Other places of concealment seemed equally obvious—under the carpet, in a drawer. In the end, she stuck it between the pages of a large black Bible that rested on the bedside table, and put Elleri's traveling clock on top of it. It was not clear why Elleri took the clock along with her, as its ticking made it ineligible to have it by her when she was trying to sleep. It was used only in the carriage. That night, the ticking kept Vanessa awake, though it had never bothered her before. For close to an hour she lay on her back, listening to the brisk tick tick and planning the next day's movements, till at last she dozed off from sheer exhaustion.

At six she went to her aunt's room to rouse her. "Leaving so soon? You're insane, child. No one leaves so early. They will take us for yahoos."

"We have to leave. Landon is here. He followed us—not difficult, as you left the instructions at the inn," Vanessa said angrily.

"Then we dare not leave. He'll only follow us again. Good God, we are doomed to spend an entire *day* with the Raffertys. I shall remain in bed. I did not close an eye the whole night long in any case, and am fatigued. Never got an instant's sleep," she claimed with that pride that is an integral part of the insomniac's makeup along with self-delusion.

"We have an escort." Vanessa went on to explain about Mr. Carlisle's fortuitous arrival at Oakdene. It was odd he had not known the estate's name. He had not, though, when she mentioned it in conversation. But it was his first visit to Edward's home; that must account for it.

Elleri asked for her mirror and brush, complained about the bags under her eyes, pulled the bell cord to request coffee in her room while she dressed, then sent Vanessa out while she surreptitiously dabbed a drop of rouge on her cheeks. In theory, she held that rouge was "common," but in practice she resorted to it when she was feeling under the weather.

Vanessa did not think to ask for coffee. She was hungry, tired and irritable when she tripped down the stairs, making as little sound as possible. Her temper did not improve to see Mr. Kiley lounging at the bottom of the stairs, conversing with Rafferty.

"So you think it is Mr. Higgins I should speak to about the potholes in the road?" he said, then turned to cast one laughing eye on Vanessa.

"Higgins is the man," Rafferty confirmed. "Ah, good morning, Miss Bradford. Mr. Kiley tells me you are in such a great hurry you will not take breakfast. I think you are foolish to go off without at least coffee, but if it is your habit, I shan't say more. You don't look as though you need to diet, to me, I must say. The young girls today all want to look like scarecrows, and succeed very well."

"Good morning, ma'am," Kiley added to her welcome. "Aren't we all early birds today? Carlisle tells me he too is going in our direction. As we are all traveling to Ipswich, I wonder if you would be kind enough to allow me to travel in your carriage? Mr. Rafferty has kindly offered to attend to having mine fixed. My axle, you know, was cracked on these *awful* roads they have around Oakdene."

"They've not been resurfaced in twenty years," Rafferty lied wildly.

"Shocking," Kiley said with deep sympathy.

"My aunt particularly dislikes company in the carriage," Vanessa said coldly.

"Unchristian *I* call it," Rafferty said with a sharp nod of the head. He walked off then, muttering about people not caring how much bother they caused others, but only let anyone ask a favor of *them,* and it was a different story.

"I am surprised Miss *Simons* is so mean," Kiley said. "I quite counted on Miss Bradford's lack of hospitality, however, and as Carlisle has not seen fit to offer me a lift, I have sent to the inn for a mount, and shall accompany you mounted."

"You can't have done so already!" she exclaimed.

Mr. Carlisle sauntered in from the breakfast room. He lifted his shoulders, giving her a helpless look behind the interloper's back.

"I am efficient," he allowed with a modest bow. She knew it to be true. He had also managed to learn her destination was Ipswich, by what means she could not know. She had not told the Raffertys, and certainly Carlisle had not told him. "It chanced I had a little business to do at the inn as well. Breakfast," he explained to Carlisle. "I had no notion of setting out on an empty stomach, and did not know the servants would be up so early. *Seven* had been mentioned as the hour for leaving," he reminded Vanessa. As he spoke, he looked at her fixedly. She didn't know what to make of it. It seemed he was trying to tell her something.

Miss Simons came complaining down the stairs, looking every inch as elegant as usual, in a neat traveling suit of blue serge. She was introduced to Carlisle, and expressed every pleasure at making his acquaintance. After struggling for several minutes over the proper mode of address for a gentleman who had changed his name overnight, she also said "Good morning, Colonel Kiley," to do honor to both personas.

She was answered by a half-swallowed gurgle of laughter from the man.

Leaving without breakfast seemed an unnecessary savagery, as Kiley was already assured of being on their trail, but as it had been settled, there was no food ready, so they went out the door, the ladies in a state of great discomfort and ire. "Why did he laugh?" Elleri enquired of her niece. "I made sure I had hit on the best greeting. Ought I to have said Mr. Landon instead?"

Carlisle walked off toward his smart yellow curricle, and Kiley waited for the ladies. Miss Simons, displeased with his lack of manners, took two steps away and stared into the distance, to show her disgust.

"News for you," he said to Vanessa. "You'll never guess the first fellow to pull into the inn after you yesterday. Mr. Carlisle. Or a fellow driving such a rig as his, in any case, and the description of the driver, too, sounded like him. A jack dandy with a smirking face was the description, verbatim. A very apt one, don't you agree?"

"What is your own rig like?" she asked.

"Why—a yellow curricle, in fact, with also a team of grays, but . . ." Carlisle's grays were dancing with impatience to be off.

"The smirking face and dandified appearance, too, so *very* apt!" Vanessa pointed out. "It was yourself he spoke of, depend upon it. He was pulling your leg." She strode off to her carriage, with Miss Simons following close behind.

"So Mr. Landon is the spy who is after our letter. A pity," Miss Simons said, glancing out the window at him. "One has such a strong feeling he would make an excellent guard, that it is a pity he is not to be trusted. Carlisle, on the other hand, looks extremely innocent, and ineffectual."

"We dare not trust either of them," Vanessa answered, worried at Landon's last comment. "We must devise some way to be rid of both of them. Oh, how I rue the day I ever met Kiley."

"There is no need to rue Carlisle, at least," Elleri consoled herself, till her niece disillusioned her with Landon's tale that he had been at the inn. She then looked out the window, to see if she could tell by the cut of their jackets which was to be abhorred. They both looked so remarkably handsome and elegant she wished she could trust them. It was very nice to have a male escort for a trip. It made stopping at the inns much more dignified, with someone to see to hiring parlors and tipping waiters and ordering wine.

"Do you know, Nessa, I have just had an idea! You were alone with Carlisle last night downstairs—*very* improper of you, by the by. Be sure you don't breathe a word to Henry or he'll snap my head off for not going with you. But what I meant is, Carlisle would have tapped you on the head and stolen the letter then, for you had it in your stocking."

"*He* didn't know that. He would be in an awkward position, having revealed himself without getting what he was after. He knew he would have better opportunities, traveling right along with us. I'm sorry I asked him."

"Yes, love, but on the other hand, if Kiley *is* a spy— you recall that French newspaper—we will be ever so glad to have someone to protect us, even if it is only Carlisle. Is the letter back in your stocking?"

"Yes," was the despondent answer. She wished she could think of a better hiding place, but was soon diverted to wishing she could have a cup of coffee instead. She tried to find some way to solve her puzzle. She had only Kiley's word for it that Carlisle had been at the inn, and she had certainly no reason to trust *him*. He only wanted her to turn Carlisle off so she would be unprotected. Carlisle knew Edward Rafferty—it could not have been arranged in any underhanded way. Of course if Carlisle *had* been at the inn, he could have learned not only where Oakdene was, but that the family boasted a son, who was not at home at that particular time. Would *anyone* be so bold? Really it was rather odd he should have offered his help on such short acquaintance, and his arrival at the house too was about right to have followed Elleri and herself from Tilbury. It was strange he had not known the name of the estate, if he had been Edward's friend since school days. On the other hand, he had not put himself forward; it was rather she who had sought his help. Certainly he was to be trusted, but never to the extent of knowing her true mission. He would remain till she was rid of Kiley, then she would reconsider the matter.

CHAPTER
Eight

*T*HE OBVIOUS TIME and place to be rid of Kiley was at their first stop, and Vanessa cudgeled her brains to think of some manner to do so. She must pretend she trusted him, invent a good story to make him think she had come to mistrust Carlisle. She would say her father had warned her in particular against a gentleman who bore some peculiar physical characteristic. She rapidly scanned her brief acquaintance with Carlisle for such an oddity—something small enough to have escaped early detection. She remembered having noticed the night before that he had a scar on his left hand, a white half-moon on the knuckle of the index finger. She would claim she did not notice it till that very morning. Next she must invent an errand to send Kiley on some errand that would take at least an hour, to give her time to evade him. This proved extremely difficult to do. She was coming to know Kiley well enough to realize he would not easily be fooled. Perhaps she could claim she was ill, and ask him to go for a doctor. . . . If she could assume a credible pallor, he would not suspect her of planning to flee.

"Auntie, do you have your talcum powder in that little night bag you carry?" she asked suddenly.

"To be sure, I have. I never travel without it. I also have my bottle of Gowland's lotion here, and rice powder and rouge—not that I ever use it! Well, *occasionally* when traveling. We ancients fade away to a ghost when we are on the road, especially when we cannot sleep." Elleri glanced to her niece. "Do you know, Nessa, I think you would be wise to use a daub of rouge this morning. I would not suggest it at home, but among *strangers* it cannot matter. You look very peaky. It would be going without proper sleep and breakfast that has done it. *One* of those gentlemen is not a spy, and they are both very elegant. There is no point wasting a chance to nab the respectable one. Here, let me put just a tiny daub of this rouge on your cheeks."

"No," Vanessa said, smiling. "I want to look as pale as possible."

"Yes, some gentlemen *do* like the fragile, consumptive sort of female, but I never thought that your style in the least."

"You misunderstood. I am about to be ill."

"What a pity! I hope you are not going to cast up your accounts. There is *nothing* so unromantic. It would be enough to turn off a hardened rake. It is bound to give them both a disgust of you. But even if you *are*, you should still use the rouge."

Vanessa outlined her scheme, patting the talcum on her cheeks as she spoke. Her aunt listened, doubtful. "That is all very well, but what if Kiley is the innocent one? Then you have turned him off, and put us in Carlisle's clutches."

"I'll think of something to get rid of him at the next stop. I am sorry I asked him along."

"*I* am sorry they are not both eligible. There is nothing like a little competition to whet a gentleman's appetite. Ah, here is Kiley pulling alongside of us now. He is definitely the more mannish of the two, but Carlisle has a more personable air."

Vanessa put down the window and stuck her head out. "I must speak to you, Colonel Landon," she said eagerly, using his preferred name, the one under which he was assumed to be innocent.

He regarded her with suspicion, then noticed she was looking very pale. "What is it?" he asked.

"It is Mr. Carlisle. I have just noticed—remembered— that is, Papa mentioned a man around Hastings whom he believed to be a French spy, and I now suspect Carlisle is the man."

Speech was difficult, between the rattle and dust from the wheels and Landon's being mounted, but she outlined the story she had invented, and looked at him for signs of having swallowed it. "Odd your father didn't mention this scar to *me*," he pointed out.

This seemed an auspicious moment to put her hand to her brow and claim a bout of nausea.

"It is having set out without anything to eat. We'll stop at the first place for something. Can you hold on for a mile or so?" he asked. She nodded her head. "Good. Keep your window open and take deep gulps of air. If you are going to be sick, let me know. I'll keep a sharp eye on you, and signal the groom to pull over."

She leaned back against the seat, while he rode alongside them for a few moments. After a while he said, "I'm going to canter ahead and see if there's anywhere close by we can stop. Are you all right for the moment?"

She nodded her head, weakly, like an invalid. He was soon back, announcing they were approaching a small hostel where they would stop. This met with her grateful approval. She summoned her thespian powers for the next step. She was happy it was not a village, but only a small wayside inn that tended to travelers. There would not be a doctor in the immediate vicinity.

Carlisle was not far behind them, but it was Landon who opened the carriage for the ladies to descend. Elleri had been given orders to inform Carlisle of the plan; she waited for him, while Landon helped Vanessa into the inn. She leaned heavily on his arm, allowing an occasional low moan to escape her lips.

"Buck up; you'll soon feel better," he encouraged, helping her gently up the steps to the door. He explained to the proprietress that the lady was unwell, and was shown into the private parlor, boasting a settee as well as table and chairs. "Lie down here till you feel more the thing," he suggested, with every appearance of genuine concern. "Where is your companion? Has she a vinaigrette?"

Elleri was still with Carlisle, explaining in her own lengthy fashion what was afoot.

"She has one with her. She'll be here presently," Vanessa said. "Before they come, Colonel, I must speak to you in private."

He went down on one knee beside the settee, examining her intently with those dark eyes. She was actually pale, and with a fairly sleepless night, had some dark circles under her eyes, so that her illness was possible to believe. "I don't understand your father sending you on such a mission as this," he said harshly.

She raised a hand to object. He immediately took it in his. "Never mind. We'll make it. I am happy you have come to trust me, Miss Bradford. You must realize the danger now, with Carlisle knowing where you are going."

"Did *he* tell you we are going to Ipswich?" she asked, ready to brain Carlisle for his loose tongue.

"No, of course not. Your father told me," he assured her, but his original thought was that they were headed to London.

She nodded, as though accepting this patent lie. "I know what is on your mind," he said, nodding with a rueful smile. "When I spoke of accompanying you to *London*, I revealed my own plan. *I* convinced Colonel Bradford London was the proper destination for your news. Is *that* why you have mistrusted me all this while?"

"Yes, of course," she said, with an apologetic glance up from under her lashes. This gave her an excellent excuse to now place her apparent confidence in him. He looked immeasurably relieved.

"What a foolish misunderstanding! All my fault too," he said, swift to exculpate. "Poor girl, what a dither I put you in. No wonder you latched onto any help that offered."

"Now I have a favor to ask you, Colonel," she said,

smiling shyly. "Will you help me to be rid of Carlisle? It was shatter-brained of me to have trusted him."

"One never looks for both brains *and* beauty in a lady," he said gallantly. "It is my job to get rid of him. Don't worry about *that*." There was some grim satisfaction in his statement. Vanessa had a fearful premonition that he was very well able to do it, too.

"How shall you accomplish it?" she asked.

"Leave that to me. The first thing is to get you back on your feet. Where *is* that woman?" he asked impatiently, with a look to the door.

Elleri Simons entered with her vinaigrette already drawn out. She replaced Landon at the settee. Miss Bradford had soon "recovered" sufficiently to sit up, at which time she put her hand to her head and moaned in anguish. "Oh, my head! I *know* I am getting one of my migraines," she wailed. "I wish there were a doctor nearby."

Landon looked pensive, then nudged Elleri aside to return to Vanessa. "You cannot be doping yourself at such a time as this," he told her. "If the pain is too severe for you to go on, give me the letter, and I'll deliver it. You can rest here with your companion in comfort and safety. I'll return as soon as the job is done."

This she had not foreseen. "We'll send Carlisle off for a doctor," he added next, rearranging all her carefully laid schemes, as she might have known he would, had she had more time to consider it. She came to see, too late, that she would never get away from him while she had the letter, and determined on the spot that she would write up a forged note for him to deliver.

"I dislike to fail Papa. I promised him I would deliver it."

"It is the spirit, not the letter, of the promise that must be followed. Whose hand passes it over to the government is irrelevant," he assured her. "Your father suggested that I do it for you, so you need not trouble your conscience on that score."

"I think if I rested half an hour and had something to eat, I would feel stout enough to go on," she countered.

"That's the girl," he complimented her, patting her

shoulder as though she were a child. "We can spare half an hour. Meanwhile, I shall lose Carlisle. I'm going around to the stable here for a better nag than the jade I got at Tilbury, while you eat. I could go in your carriage with you, but would feel better if we had a mount besides, just in case . . ."

"In case what?" she asked, curious, and also relieved he did not plan to sit in their carriage.

"In case of attack by a highwayman. I shall act as scout—ride ahead from time to time, and on horseback, it is also possible to canter up to a hilltop, when one offers, to view the countryside. As a colonel's daughter, you must be familiar with reconnaissance missions," he mentioned.

He was no sooner out the door than she called for paper and pen, and, folding a perfectly blank sheet up, she addressed the envelope to Sir Giles Harkman, in the best forgery of her father's hand that she could contrive. She had no seal, but this could not be helped. With a frowning look at her work, she took it and squeezed it into a tight ball, then smoothed it out between her fingers, to give it the worn air of the original. This done, she tucked it into the bodice of her gown. Carlisle, caught to listen to her aunt, looked in her direction from time to time but did not come to her. She ordered bread, butter and coffee, which made her feel rather worse than better, owing to her excitement.

When Kiley returned, she called him to her side, away from the others, who took coffee at the table near the fireplace. "I have thought over what you suggested, Colonel," she said in a conspiratorial whisper, "and have decided the following. I shall give you the letter to take to Sir Giles, if you will promise *not* to take it to London. I shall stay here an hour or so to keep Carlisle busy, while you run ahead with it. We shall meet there, at Ipswich. Agreed?"

She deemed Kiley a consummate actor when he frowned his disapproval of this plan, instead of snatching at it, as she knew he wanted to do.

"I have two objections," he said. "London is closer, and the logical place to take the news. Any fears it will not receive close attention are groundless when I deliver the letter personally. The other is that it leaves you unprotected with Carlisle. He is not so toothless a tiger as he looks. That boyish charm hides a rather nasty nature, to judge by his knocking you on the head at the inn. He might think you have the letter, and do you some serious injury. I would feel derelict in my duty to leave you alone with him. But of course delivering the letter is the prime mission. He won't believe for one minute I have gone off without it, however. In the worst case, you can tell him I have got it. He'll go after me, and leave you in peace.''

"I am not afraid of *him*. Of greater concern to me is where you take the letter. I promised Papa it would go to Ipswich.''

"All right—I'll take it there for you. There is time. I cannot just walk peacefully out, after being at such pains to have joined your party. How shall we arrange my departure?'' He spoke hurriedly, in his eagerness to achieve his end. A youthful smile alit on his harsh face. "But of course! We shall have a fight. In the heat of my temper, I stomp out. Carlisle will suspect I am lurking around the closest corner, and think little of it. The battle causes a recrudescence of your migraine—how is it, by the by?''

"Much better. It was the hunger that caused it.''

"Good. You shall have a migraine *quand même,* and send Carlisle off for a sawbones, while you and your aunt dart back to Raffertys. It will be a dead bore for you, but perfectly safe. He won't think of looking for you there, do you think? Even if he does, you can tell them what is happening, and they won't let him in. Oakdene looks a strongish fortress. The letter will be safe in my keeping, so you need not worry about that end of it. What do you think?''

She thought it an acceptable plan. Carlisle was not to be sent off till after Kiley had left, and once he was gone, there was no need to send him at all unless she wanted to. That decision could await. She had no intention, of course, of returning to Raffertys. She must get hold of a map and find another route to Ipswich, at all speed. "Fine,'' she said, smiling with contentment.

"I am very happy we got all this business straightened out at last. I look forward to meeting you under less harassing circumstances at a later date, Miss Bradford." He allowed a little smile to lighten his eyes, and a lingering glance to settle on her face, but soon his eagerness prevailed and he said, "May I have the letter, then?"

"You'll have to turn away while I extract it," she answered. She found, to her consternation, that she was blushing.

"So *that's* where it is," he said, laughing, but very softly, so as not to call Carlisle's attention. He turned his head aside obediently while she pulled the letter out, warm and crumpled.

He took it, read the address, turned it over. "No seal?" he asked, surprised.

"Papa was in such a rush, he must have forgotten," she said, looking at the envelope. Then she smiled her prettiest smile at him, which had the desired effect of drawing his attention from the envelope.

"Where shall we meet?" he asked as he surreptitiously put the letter in his inside jacket pocket, with a quick look to Carlisle to see he was not watching. "You'll stay at Raffertys, will you? I suppose you *could* go back to Levenhurst without danger."

"What do *you* think best, Colonel? You have more experience than I in these matters."

He saw nothing amiss in this blatant flattery. There was even a touch of satisfaction about him. "Stay with the Raffertys," he decided. "It will not be pleasant, but it will be safe. I want you to be safe. I *did* promise Colonel Bradford to look after you, you know. Now that I have come to know you a little better, I find I would dislike it very much if anything were to happen to you." He looked at her a long moment with a smile that it was difficult to read, but that she soon decided he regularly used to con women, as he had got it down so pat. She actually felt a flush of pleasure at his open admiration.

"Whatever you say," she answered meekly.

He cocked his head. "That's quite an about-face from your attitude last night."

"I did not quite trust you then," she reminded him.

"That was wise of you. To distrust *everyone*, I mean. A pity you had not saved some of your suspicion for Carlisle. Never mind. We'll take care of him." He reached out and squeezed her fingers. "Ready for the battle royal?" he asked. "We are about to come to serious cuffs, you and I, to give me an excuse to depart. I hope he doesn't find it too odd."

He arose abruptly to stand glaring down at her. In a loud, angry voice, he said, "I have been called a lot of things in my time, but this is too much!"

She blinked in surprise, and hastily considered some line to match this violent beginning. "Well, it's true!" she exclaimed sharply. "You *are* an impostor. Calling yourself a colonel one minute, and Mr. Kiley the next. You are a crook, sir, and so I tell you. If you pester me one moment longer, I shall call a constable."

He glowered over her, as though in a rage. "As to calling a constable, he might be interested in your *other* traveling companion, the gentleman who *calls* himself Mr. Carlisle." On this speech, he turned on his heel and departed the room.

This alteration in plans had to be explained to her companions as soon as he was gone.

"Famous, Miss Bradford. You are up to anything!" Carlisle congratulated her. "Now we can proceed unhindered to Ipswich. Oh, this is much more exciting than going to a gaming hell with Edward Rafferty. I would not have missed it for anything. Gather up your diamonds, and let us be off."

She hastily considered developing a migraine and getting rid of Carlisle while she was about it. But he looked so perfectly innocent, smiling and speaking of Edward Rafferty in a way to make her think they were indeed old friends, that she took the quick decision to go on with him. His next speech confirmed her as to the rightness of her course. "There's a back road that jogs toward Maldon—it is not so well surfaced as the other, but it cuts a few miles off the trip. We haven't gotten rid of Kiley that easily. He'll be skulking around Chelmsford, looking out for us. I don't doubt we'll arrive before him, as he is riding that wretched old nag from the inn. He's out in his luck if he thought to hire something better here.. There isn't a piece of horseflesh to be had. I checked.''

It was good to have a man to make these practical decisions in a way that was difficult for two inexperienced ladies. Vanessa would have wasted precious time poring over maps, and then probably have taken the wrong route. She was happy too to learn Kiley had not got a better mount.

"Let us go," she said, arising to place her hand on Mr. Carlisle's arm. Elleri did the same on his left arm, but he stopped them. "Hadn't one of us better pay the shot here?" he asked, laughing. "Innkeepers are so dreadfully commercial. They want to be paid for their services." As he spoke, he pulled out his purse and called a servant, overriding all their polite objections. His every move was so polite and gentlemanly it was very hard to let any suspicion remain. As the ladies joggled along a road noticeably inferior to the main road, they were agreed they had acted very wisely in the matter.

"And even if that nice Mr. Carlisle *does* turn out to be a rogue," Miss Simons declared, "I am sure *you* will handle him, minx, for you are up to all the rigs. I never knew what a cunning actress you were, till today."

Flushed with victory, Vanessa tended to agree. She had handled Kiley pretty well. It was not for a quarter of an hour that it occurred to her that if he were truly a spy, he would have that letter ripped open as soon as he was out of their sight. He would be back hounding them, but at least then she would know unequivocally that he was the enemy. If, on the other hand, he did *not* return, she had deprived herself of a real helper, the man sent to her by her father. Reconsidering the whole case against him, she conceded that his stories *could* be true. Her father *could* have sent him to her without giving him any identification; he *could* have talked Papa into sending the letter directly to London; he *could* even have had a French newspaper in his possession without being a French spy. And if he were innocent, then Carlisle was likely guilty. Someone had knocked her out and searched her body for the letter. Was it possible she had placed herself undefended in the enemy's hands? She would soon know, as soon as Kiley caught up with them again. And if he had not done so by Chelmsford, then she would know Carlisle was the spy, and take whatever steps occurred to her. The remainder of the time was spent in conjuring with which "steps" to accomplish this end.

CHAPTER
Nine

*T*HE MORNING PASSED in this troublesome fashion. The weather at least was good—bright and warm, and while the road was not so well surfaced as the main route, neither was there heavy traffic to slow them down, nor such an absolute lack of vehicles as to feel dangerously isolated. Carlisle had spoken of reaching Maldon for luncheon, but with an early start and a light breakfast, they were more than ready to take a break when they were still two miles short of the town.

"Just as well to stay away from the cities," Carlisle pointed out when he had pulled alongside their stopped carriage. "If Kiley takes into his head to come looking for us, he is less likely to find us at a small spot like this."

"Do you think he will do so?" Miss Simons asked.

"He isn't likely to give up on a diamond necklace only because Miss Bradford threatened to call a constable on him, is he?" he asked. "He is setting some trap probably. He thought we would be following shortly behind him. If we're lucky, he'll cool his heels at Chelmsford, waiting for us to come along."

This picture was amusing enough to set them all smiling as they descended to have their carriage and curricle stabled at the small roadside in. "We'll have a quick bite and be well north of Colchester before we stop for the night," Carlisle said, lending his arm to the ladies to mount the brick stairs to the doorway.

The small hostelry boasted no private dining room, but in such an out-of-the-way spot, and before the common lunch hour, there were no other customers. They ate cold meat and cheese, to save waiting for hot food. They were just finishing their coffee, prior to leaving, when the front door of the establishment opened. Vanessa felt a churning of apprehension within her chest. She knew instinctively who it would be, knew now for a certainty he was the enemy. Within thirty seconds, Mr. Kiley's tall form loomed in the doorway of the dining room, his face a black scowl.

"A clever trick, miss, but you will have to get up earlier than six o'clock to fool *me!*" he said angrily.

She laid down her cup and regarded him with a calmness that taxed her acting ability. "I cannot imagine what you mean, sir. I threatened to call a constable if you did not leave me alone. I thought you had heeded my warning, but as you have not, I shall summon him here if you direct one more word to me."

"You don't get away that easily."

"Try if you can stop me," she answered. She pushed back her chair and arose majestically. Carlisle jumped to his feet in a belated effort to come to her assistance. Kiley looked as if he would like to say a deal more, but something held him back. She half wished he *would* do something to enable her to have him placed under arrest. Carlisle threw a bill on the table, and with an insolent stare at the intruder, ushered the ladies from the room.

Kiley sat down and ordered a tall glass of ale. When it arrived, he walked to the window and drank it there, watching to see which direction the party took. He frowned to see Carlisle stop to scribble a note and send it off with a stable boy.

"What is that you are doing, Mr. Carlisle?" Vanessa asked.

"I am sending a note to the constable in Maldon to take a tour along this road, just in case we have any trouble with Kiley," he explained.

"A wise precaution," Elleri Simons said. "He looked ready to kill us all."

As soon as they had left, Kiley was out the door after them, without waiting till he had eaten. He looked to see their direction, then sent for a fresh mount.

When the carriage and the curricle had taken the first bend in the road, Carlisle pulled ahead and signaled for them to stop. He alit and went to their door. "I have been thinking about what Kiley said, back at the inn. What did he mean, Miss Bradford, a clever trick?" he asked, with natural curiosity.

She was strongly tempted to tell him all her business, but remembered her father's warnings. "I suppose he refers to our change of route," she answered. "He must have been looking for us along the other road."

"He has plenty of brass to as much as tell you his plan," Carlisle answered, looking dissatisfied. He regarded Vanessa with a close scrutiny. "Are you sure you're being quite frank with me, ma'am?" he asked with a trace of diffidence. "Come now, can't you trust me? I know you come from Hastings, where your father, a colonel, is active in the defense against Napoleon's probable invasion. If you are engaged in some more important job than delivering diamonds, I think you ought to tell me."

"Oh," she said, distress on every line of her face, that he had hit upon her secret. She had never had to decide anything more important than what gown to wear, or what gentleman to stand up with at a ball. Her whole life had been sheltered, giving her no opportunity to become decisive. While she hesitated, he spoke on.

"I thought as much! I shan't pry. It is none of my concern, except to do what I can to see you make your trip safely. I *do* wish you had trusted me completely," he added with a little offended glance.

"I do," she assured him. "Truly I do, it is only that Papa said—said not to trust anyone, or tell anyone, you see."

"Is it a *verbal* message you carry?" he asked.

She looked at him, unable to suppress a little jab of suspicion at the question. "What I wish to discover is just how great a danger you are in," he pointed out. "If you carry some documents, that is one thing. You may be held up and robbed of them, but if you carry the message in your head—well, that is a different matter entirely, isn't it? A much more dangerous spot for you to be in, and greater precautions must be taken for your safety. I come to see this Kiley does not mean to give up."

"He can't do anything in broad daylight," she pointed out. "Let us get back on the main road at once, before he comes after us."

"The constable should be along shortly," Elleri reminded them.

"You haven't answered my question," he said. "You have trusted me this far. Tell me the rest, and let me decide what must be done to protect you and the message." He looked worried, and completely innocent, with his frank blue eyes and open face.

She knew if she admitted she carried a letter, he would want it to safeguard himself, and her desire was to retain it on her own body. "The message is inside my head," she told him. He turned a shade paler, and looked extremely worried.

"Write it down and let me deliver it. You too carry this message in your head, Miss Simons?"

"Fiddlesticks!" was Miss Simons' answer, given with an impatient, accusing glance at her niece. "Mr. Carlisle has been a great help to us, Nessa, and it is time to tell him the truth."

He nodded his head. "I see. You *still* don't trust me," he said to Vanessa. "I had better travel in your carriage, and bring my pistol along with me." The ladies exchanged a frightened look but made no demur. Carlisle went to his curricle and extracted from under the seat a black leather pistol case.

"It is odd he happened to have a pistol with him," Vanessa said, her brow furrowing.

"Thank your lucky stars he has. You may be sure that

villain of a Kiley, or colonel, or whoever he is, has one,'' Miss Simons answered.

''Lucky I had this along with me,'' Carlisle said as he came back to them. ''I hardly ever carry a pistol, but Edward Rafferty and I had planned a spot of shooting at Manton's Gallery in London. Let us go at once.''

He opened the door of the carriage and hopped in without bothering to have the step let down. The pistol, still in its case, was stowed in the side pocket of the carriage, where its bulge brought less assurance of safety than dread that it might have to be used. Carlisle's tiger happily took over the reins of the curricle, and was the happiest member of the party for the next several miles. Within the closed carriage, spirits were low. Carlisle was naturally curious to discover where the message was secreted. He was quite as persistent as Kiley in the matter. At length Vanessa said, to silence his questions, ''I have it hidden under the lining of my valise. It is quite safe. One would have to know exactly where it is to find it. The lining has been glued back over it.''

She was becoming uneasy at his hard questioning. Doubts began to assail her as to his trustworthiness, but once she had told him her lie as to where it was hidden, he settled down to lighter conversation.

''I had to know, you know, in case anything happened to you. I don't wish to frighten you unnecessarily,'' he added apologetically. ''I shall do everything in my power to see nothing *does* happen, but it is best to be prepared for any contingency.''

''Yes,'' she agreed, and settled back to try to relax.

''Let us speak of other things,'' he said, trying manfully to amuse them, but his next speech was hardly one to bring ease. ''Is Kiley following us? I hope the constable I sent for has stopped him.''

They looked back down the road, where the dust from his curricle whirled into a cloud with that from their own carriage, making the view very murky indeed.

''We cannot very well forbid him the highway,'' he went on. ''Don't worry. I can handle him.'' He glanced to the bulging side pocket, while Miss Simons fanned herself with her gloves and wondered what she was doing, mixed up in such desperate goings-on. She had not thought of the ball since morning. How very odd!

The afternoon dragged on more slowly than the morning. There was a constant peering out the back window to see if Kiley was coming. With the denser traffic of the main thoroughfare, it was impossible to tell, but when they stopped to change team and take a glass of wine in mid-afternoon, he was observed to enter the yard not long after them. When they left, he drained his glass.

"Can't we do something to lose him?" Miss Simons begged their escort. "My nerves are on edge, always seeing him there behind us, hovering like a vulture."

"He hasn't *done* anything," Carlisle pointed out. "If he so much as *speaks* to either of you at the next stop, I shall beat him. Or call a constable," he added, perhaps more realistically. Carlisle was well enough set up, but a few inches shorter than Kiley, and smaller across the chest.

"I *know* he will break into our room again tonight," Miss Bradford worried. During the trip, she had told Carlisle of her being hit on the head and searched.

"By God, he won't, if I have to sleep outside your door with a pistol in my hands," he said hotly. "Is there no friend in the area you can go to, as you did the Raffertys last night?"

"No one. He would only make an excuse and barge in after us if we did. Maybe we had best get a fresh team and travel all night," she suggested. She was immediately talked down by her aunt, who raised the same objection as the previous night, with the same result.

"Why don't you let *me* keep the valise that holds the letter?" Carlisle asked. "I hesitated to suggest it when it was diamonds you spoke of, but a letter is another matter. I could have no possible interest in it, except to see it safely delivered. Kiley would not likely look for it in my safekeeping.

"An excellent idea," Miss Simons thought.

As the valise was innocent of anything but her clothing, Vanessa agreed to it. This was the plan set on. He would take the valise, guard it with his life, while still keeping an eye on the ladies from the next room. It was their hope to get three rooms all in a row, possibly even adjoining.

"We must stop in a city, where a constable is within easy call," Nessa insisted.

"That means Colchester," Carlisle said. "We had hoped to get a little farther before we stopped."

"No, I won't be stranded in some country inn on a dark road, away from civilization," she insisted.

"By all means, stop at Colchester. My head will split wide open if I don't get out of this carriage soon," Elleri moaned. "We are certain to get rooms there. If we go past it, there is no saying we will be in luck. We might end up driving through the dark . . ." She gave an involuntary shiver.

"Both the Red Lion and the Three Cups, at Colchester, are decent places," Carlisle mentioned.

"I have eaten at the Three Cups," Elleri said, nodding her approval. "They have a fine Renaissance dining room, with a musicians' gallery all around. I wonder if they still have music."

"This is not a social outing," her niece reminded her.

They stopped at the Red Lion, an old half-timbered inn. They could not get exactly those accommodations they wanted. Carlisle had to take a room across the hall, but for the women, a pair of adjoining rooms was hired. When the clerk shoved the register toward them, Vanessa reached for the pen, and wrote "Miss Forrester." With a sly smile, Elleri inscribed in her dainty hand "Mrs. Forrester" below it. "I know what put that name in your head, sly puss." She laughed.

"I just wanted to put some other name than our own," Vanessa said.

"That will be the White Rose Suite, ladies," the clerk said, handing them their keys.

"I'll take up the valises," Carlisle said. "I signed myself up as Mr. Pettigrew. I assume it was your hope to fool Kiley by using an alias."

"Yes, of course it was."

"You had better give me your valise," he reminded her.

"Let me get my nightclothes out of it first," she said, to allow opportunity to rip up a corner of the lining and glue a paper under it, to give an air of authenticity to her story. And where was she to get glue at a public inn?

It was better luck than she expected when the serving wench told her she would bring up a bottle.

"I hope our luck is changing," she said wistfully to her aunt.

"You'll change your mind when you try that bed," was the glum reply. "The mattress is stuffed with sticks and stones."

"I could sleep tonight if it were stuffed with needles. How *tired* I am, and I haven't done a thing all day but sit in a well-sprung chaise."

"We have worried. Worry is the most fagging thing in the world. Worry and pain." She went on to issue several instances of friends whose health and appearance had been ravaged by these twin destroyers. While she complained, Vanessa did what she had to do to her valise, then waited for the glue to dry. She walked to the window and looked out, trying for a glimpse of Kiley. The inn was built around a courtyard, where horses were being walked to and fro. Behind it was a bowling green. There was an open gallery built around the courtyard, up one story, just beyond her window, but there was no door to reach it from her room. Access was from the two ends of the hall. She would have enjoyed a stroll along it, to take the cooling air, but it would only advertise her presence if Kiley *should* happen to enter that courtyard.

"I'll just leave my clock here with you, my dear, and take my valise into my own chamber," Elleri said. "Change into your light-green frock. It goes well with your eyes. I shall do something to your hair. I *do* wish we had got it cut before coming. I shall do it after we get to Harkmans. I wonder if there are any nice young gentlemen around Ipswich," she added, her thoughts already channeling themselves into the old familiar themes.

"Have you taken Carlisle in aversion so soon?" Vanessa asked. "I made sure his taking such good care of us would incline you to give him my hand."

"That must depend on how he is situated financially. All we know thus far is that he has a place in the Cotswold Hills. Gentlemen more usually have a small hunting box there, you must know. It could be nothing more than a hunting cottage he has. It was the Cotswolds he mentioned, was it not?"

"Yes, how long ago it seems, way last night."

Water was brought up. They bathed the dust of travel from their bodies before outfitting themselves in clean gowns for the dinner with Mr. Carlisle.

"How pleasant to have a quiet evening to look forward to," Elleri said, smiling. "I shall insist on paying for dinner. I'll tell them to put it on our bill. We are falling too deep into Mr. Carlisle's debt. Henry would not like it. Be sure you don't tell him." This was her solution to anything which the colonel would dislike. To keep him in ignorance of it.

Carlisle came for the valise. "My tiger is to stay with it locked in my room while we eat. He is completely reliable. He won't let anyone in." He said this before noticing the changed gowns and refreshed coiffures.

"How lovely you both look," he said. "I will be the envy of the place, having *two* such belles to escort. Shall we go below, ladies? I have spoken for a private parlor."

"You think of everything, sir," Elleri complimented, wondering how she could tacitly tell the waiter to put the charge on her bill.

Vanessa smiled her approval. She was looking forward to dinner with him. He seemed a lively and effectual gentleman. If only she could be sure an even more effectual one would not intrude to spoil their evening. She had the liveliest dread that he would. She was correct.

CHAPTER
Ten

CARLISLE CONSIDERED HIMSELF the ladies' host, and seemed intent on being a good one. He had the private parlor waiting, with a bottle of wine ready to be served. He had scanned the menu and suggested for their delectation the ham and fowl, as mutton was too heavy for this weather. Fresh fruit and cheese he had selected for their dessert, which was quickly changed to a richer pastry at the slightest hint. How he had contrived all this while also making a careful toilette was a matter of interest to Miss Simons, who thought she had the art down to a speed not often equaled by others, but he had certainly outstripped her. On top of it, he did not appear rushed or flustered as he outlined his arrangements. She was convinced no mere owner of a hunting box could be so efficient.

They ordered dinner, then sat sipping a glass of wine while awaiting its arrival. "I assure you the letter is being guarded as I outlined, and that is the last word we shall say of its existence this evening," he promised. "By tomorrow it will be delivered safely to Ipswich, and we can relax, with the satisfaction of a job well done."

"Here, here," Miss Simons approved, lightly tapping her glass on the tabletop. "We must not lose track of each other afterward, Mr. Carlisle. You shall come to visit us whenever you are in the vicinity of Hastings."

"I will certainly avail myself of that kind offer," he told her, then turned to cast a quizzical smile at Vanessa, who had not seconded the offer. "If Miss Bradford does not object, that is?"

"Forgive me. I was wool-gathering. We will be delighted to receive you at any time."

"Do you not think we might be on a first-name basis, now that we are partners in adventure?" he asked. "We shall ask Miss Simons to decree on the propriety of it. Miss Simons, what do you say?"

He meant the question for no more than a formality, but soon learned she dealt the matter more careful consideration. She began ticking off on her fingers the length of their acquaintance—in hours, weighing against this what time to allow for the particular importance of their joint mission. "In the normal way it would not do at all," she said, shaking her head. "Not at all the thing, but then, when we have to speak of spies and fights and calling constables, it *does* seem rigid to be forever saying Mr. Carlisle, or Miss Bradford, though you must not call *me* Elleri."

While he was behind the chaperone's back to refill their glasses, he smiled at Vanessa, a boyish smile that laughed at the antique notions of the elderly. "True, the nature of our relationship must be taken into consideration," he agreed. "Were I to say, for instance, 'Duck, Miss Bradford—there is a bullet coming toward you,' only look at the time I should waste. What should I say instead? Vanessa, I believe, is the name I hear Miss Simons use. You do not hear mine, but if you did, it would be Harvey."

"Harvey," Miss Simons repeated consideringly. "It has quite a formal sound to it. I think we might call Mr. Carlisle 'Harvey,' Vanessa," she decreed.

"May I call Miss Bradford 'Vanessa' as well?" he persisted.

"Yes, you may," he was told, "but you ought not to call her Nessa till after we are a little better acquainted."

"I hope that will not be too long," he replied, with a bow divided between the pair of them.

Having dispensed with talk of their mutual business, he was intent on turning the conversation toward furthering the intimacy. This met with approval from the chaperone, all of it done quite properly under her own eye, but she missed a few meaningful looks and smiles that passed behind her back. The younger lady soon discovered it was more than friendship he had in mind. He was trying to set up a flirtation with her. An attractive and eligible girl, she was not unaccustomed to dalliance, but there was some intentness in Carlisle's advances that surprised her. Surely he had not fallen in love with her so quickly, but over dinner, while Elleri was busy cutting her meat or examining her vegetables, there were soft looks bestowed on her charge, gazings with a complete disregard for his food, then a sudden jolt of surprise would cross his face, as he blushed and attacked the food on his plate with vigor, making it clear he had been ignoring it. The only suitor to have shown his admiration so openly and naively before was a young ensign at the Army base, a mere callow youth. Vanessa had to smile to see Carlisle so smitten. He was no green youth either, but a gentleman well into his twenties.

After dinner, he suggested cards to pass a few hours before retiring. Every effort was made to be amusing, but still some pall hung over the party. Its reason was no secret to any of them. They avoided mentioning it, but each silently wondered whether Kiley would not come pouncing in on them. Carlisle frequently took a nervous peek out the window—every time he heard wheels or hooves. Miss Simons played her hand of cards so poorly that she trumped herself, while Nessa declared after one hand that she did not feel much like cards tonight. She would just watch them, but she listened at the door into the hallway more than she watched.

"I had better take a run up to my room to see everything

is all right," Harvey said a little later on. It was a relief to get it out into the open, that they were all worried.

"I wish you would," Vanessa said.

He was gone rather a long time, long enough for them to become worried. Vanessa stood at the parlor door, looking out for his return. She was still there when Kiley strode into the inn. He looked extremely angry, and very dirty. He was grimed with dust, and mud, which had hardened in the sun to solid buttons of dirt, bespattered his boots and trousers. His shirt too had dark marks on it. Even a hard ride mounted on horseback could hardly account for his condition. He looked as though he had been rolling in filth. Miss Simons expressed a timid hope that the inn would not hire a room to anyone so disreputable-looking. As they watched, however, the register was pushed toward him for him to sign in.

Just before he went to the stairway, he directed one long scowl toward them. "Good evening, the Misses Forrester," he called across the few intervening yards. "I will do myself the honor to join you presently." Then he turned and walked quickly up the stairs.

"Surely he ought to have called us the Misses Forrester," Miss Simons thought. "Certainly it would be written so— though it would be more proper to say Miss Forrester and Miss Vanessa—or . . . I am sure I signed *Mrs*. Forrester." She trailed off into doubt.

"Shouldn't we warn Harvey?" Vanessa asked. She was not surprised Kiley had come. The only surprise was that it had taken him so long. From his condition, she knew his interval had not been dull, nor pleasant.

"He should be down presently. If he is not, we shall send a servant up to see what is going on," Miss Simons decided. "Oh, dear, I was never so vexed in my life. What an evening it has been, trying to keep up any polite conversation, and the only thing in any of our heads that pesty man, though it would not do to *harp* on it, when that nice Harvey is trying so very hard to be entertaining. He is well bred, a true gentleman. It is under such trying circumstances as this that breeding shows, trying to talk under stress." To her, this was the important matter of their evening.

"I believe that is carrying breeding to a foolish excess," Nessa replied.

"There can be no excess of breeding!"

Carlisle was soon back. "You saw him?" he asked. They nodded.

"What took you so long? Was something the matter?" Vanessa asked.

"I thought it was Kiley I spotted from my window, and waited to be sure. You ladies go to your rooms, and let me deal with him. You will not want to be bothered with him."

"Excellent!" Miss Simons agreed instantly.

"I am not afraid of him. I'll stay," Nessa said. This was not quite true. She *was* frightened, but it was an exhilarating fright, carrying with it some desire to lock horns again with the enemy.

"There might be violence, Nessa," her aunt pointed out. "It would be improper for you to be mixed up in it—to see it, I mean."

"She is right, Vanessa," Harvey urged. "I'll take care of him, and go up to you ladies in your room after."

These offers of "dealing" with Kiley and "taking care" of him sounded well enough, but it was not at all clear whether Kiley would be dealt with or do the dealing. With this in doubt, Vanessa decided her first duty was to safeguard the letter. She must leave the field of battle to the men, much as she disliked to do it.

"Come along, then," Elleri urged. "Thank you ever so much, Harvey. So very kind of you," she rattled on, easing herself out the door and out of trouble. She scampered up the stairs as fast as her legs could carry her. "So fortunate Harvey was looking out his window and spotted Kiley."

"It took him long enough to come down after he *did* spot him. You would think he would have arrived sooner—come darting down the instant he knew it was Kiley."

"You forget, dear, he *thinks* he has your letter. He was likely hiding the valise somewhere."

"That is true. How ungrateful of me, after all his trouble. The truth is, I find his company strangely wearing after a while."

"It is the nerves. I made sure we had been at cards for hours, when I saw by my watch it was only twenty-five minutes."

The next forty-five minutes passed even more slowly, waiting in their room for Harvey to come to them. Once a minute, one or the other of them would tiptoe to the door and ease it open silently, to see if either of the men was in the hallway, coming or going, or possibly fighting the other. They concluded Kiley had a light step, for he had managed to get downstairs without attracting their attention. At the end of their vigil, Carlisle came to them, unharmed and smiling. Miss Simons entertained a doubt that she did the proper thing to have him step into her chamber, knew she did wrong to close the door, but did it anyway.

"Well, and what happened?" she asked eagerly.

"I have convinced him he is on a fool's errand," he told them, beaming at his cleverness. "He thinks we are eloping, you and I, Vanessa."

"What!" Miss Simons squealed. "Oh, Harvey—Mr. Carlisle, that was ill done. If word of it ever gets out, Nessa is ruined."

Harvey looked to his victim with apologetic horror. "I'm sorry! Indeed I didn't mean to create any mischief for you. I only wanted to help."

"That's all right, Harvey. No harm done," Vanessa said, yet she was extremely annoyed with this puppy. She certainly did not want Kiley to think she had chosen him for a husband, but of course Kiley did not think anything of the sort. He had only pretended to believe the foolish story to lessen Carlisle's vigilance. If Harvey was stupid enough to think he had conned Kiley, he was of very little use to her. She needed a sharper ally than that.

"He is to spend the night here at the inn," Harvey went on. "It is getting pretty late, you know, and he has a jaded nag on his hands, as well as being exhausted himself from riding all day. I don't believe he'll bother us again. We'll leave early in the morning, before he is awake. I hope you won't be even more angry with me, Miss Simons, but I told him you are helping us with the elopement, chaperoning your niece till we reach the border. We are headed north, you see, so it is credible we could be off to Gretna Green."

"We would be headed toward the Great North Road if we were going to Scotland," Vanessa said, rather curtly.

Miss Simons' attention was on another matter. "Why did you not tell him Nessa is to be married from the home of friends?" she asked. "It would be much more respectable—not to say it is respectable, but it is less ramshackle than being wed over the anvil. No one will ever believe it of me, Mr. Carlisle. I'm afraid that was left out of your reckoning. I would be the last lady to countenance a runaway match for my niece."

"I don't suppose Kiley knows you well enough to realize that," he mentioned. "I'm sorry if I have made a botch of it. If I have ruined Vanessa's reputation, I will be ready—willing—*happy* to make restitution. I mean . . ."

"You are very sweet"—Nessa smiled at him—"but I don't think I am quite ruined, Harvey."

"Oh," he said, rather sadly.

When Elleri tumbled to what he was saying, a tender expression took over her face. She looked from one to the other of them, nodding. "If she is ruined, we know what to do about it, then," she said archly, and taking Carlisle by the elbow, propelled him toward the door, said good night and closed it behind him, before turning to Vanessa with a quizzing look.

"Well, miss, you have certainly conquered *that* young man in a hurry. How well done of him! As good as an offer. We must hear more of that property in the Cotswolds tomorrow. Carlisle—I wonder if he is related to the Howards, the Earl of Carlisle. Ah, but then he would be a Howard, would he not? To say nothing of being a Catholic. Still, it is a good name. Harvey Carlisle. Vanessa Carlisle," she said in an experimental way, to test its euphony.

"Kiley was not so easily taken in," Vanessa said, cutting into her monologue.

"You may be sure he was. People are always ready to believe the worst of a girl. I only hope he does not tell anyone."

"He knows what we are doing. He opened that envelope I gave him. He is a dangerous, clever spy, and Mr. Carlisle is a fool. I wonder what Kiley is up to now."

"Let us hope he is not broadcasting your elopement, in spite."

"We would be better off, safer, if he were."

"How can you say such a thing! So very shabby."

Vanessa turned off her ears, realizing she had two fools for cohorts. If the letter was to be safely delivered, it was up to herself alone.

CHAPTER
Eleven

MISS SIMONS RATTLED on for a long time on such irrelevant topics as choices for a honeymoon spot, and where the trousseau should be made up. It left Vanessa free to worry and plan in peace. She was only twenty-five miles from Ipswich. It could not be impossible to get there safely, if she used her wits. The great danger was that Kiley knew her destination, would be laying traps for her along the way. It seemed safer to dart off in some other direction, to fool him. As much as she disliked to strike out alone, she was coming to think it would throw him off the track. If she could find a good disguise, then go in some other direction than Ipswich, she might evade him. But what direction? London was farther, but it was still within a day's travel. There was the whole Foreign Office there that could handle the matter for her. Yes, she would buy or steal some man's clothing, hire a hack, as Kiley would be looking for her in a carriage, and ride to London, with Gretch and his pistol for company. Or should they go on a public coach? The mail coach was fast. He would not dare to assault her in front of half a dozen travelers, and on His Majesty's Mail Coach.

"But you must not breathe a word of it to Henry," Miss Simons terminated her speech, looking sharp to see this was understood.

"Tell him what?" Vanessa asked, shaking to attention.

"My dear, you have not heard a *word* I have been saying. Your head is full of Harvey. It is only to be expected, at such a romantic time. Of course he will make a *proper* offer later, after speaking to Henry."

Nessa smiled, to encourage Elleri to chatter on in this harmless way. When should she make her departure was the next question she posed herself. Not in the dangerous darkness of night, yet daylight was too revealing. He could be belowstairs at the crack of dawn, watcing out for her. When—when—*when?*

"Something old, something new—I shall buy you a new veil, Nessie. Your mama's is perfectly yellow, practically *brown,* in fact. I had it out of the trunk last week. Is not that a strange coincidence?"

Elleri's mindless chatter disturbed her concentration. She must get her to go to her own room and close the door, to allow her to ring for a servant and arrange the purchase of clothing for the masquerade. She would not take breakfast in the morning. She would leave at dawn, down the back stairs, disguised as a boy, send word to have the groom awaiting her. No, she would open her window and leave by the balcony that ran around the rear wall of the inn. Kiley had spies, some boy he hired to report on goings-on in the stable. She knew that from their stop at Tilbury. She would not go to the inn stable here, then, but hire a mount at another hostelry in town. In fact, it would be safer in the long run not even to take her groom with her. Kiley knew him by sight, and to masquerade him as well as herself was too monumental a task. Kiley would be watching her door, so she would leave by the window and get a good head start on him.

"The Phillipses will never come all the way from Scotland, but there is no reason you and Harvey could not go north for the honeymoon, to see them," Elleri said, looking to her niece for a reaction to this suggestion.

"I have a ripping headache," Vanessa said. "Do you mind if we go to bed now?"

"An excellent idea. I think better lying down. I can make the arrangements better in bed than anywhere else. I'll just plan it all mentally, and jot it down after we are through with this dreadful trip. I see the whole of the arranging will be left up to me. *You* are so distracted it is clear you are thinking only of Harvey."

On this speech, she went into her room, and left the door open. In five minutes, Nessa blew out her light, and went to say good night, carefully closing the door behind her. Then she rang the bell to bring a servant up to her. For the inordinate sum of three pounds, it was arranged the servant would smuggle a young gentleman's jacket, trousers, hat and boots to her at five o'clock the next morning, doing the whole in a stealthy manner, looking out for and avoiding any observers. It remained only to see to the letter's safekeeping for the rest of the night. With that balcony running right past her window, and with Kiley in the inn, she did not feel at all secure. She checked to make sure the window was locked. Access could only be gained by breaking the glass, which would cause enough noise to bring help. But just in case, she examined the room for a secure hiding place.

Nothing seemed right. In the end, she folded the letter in half lengthwise, opened up the end of the curtain's hem, and inserted it. It caused the hem to stick out at an odd angle, but in a dark corner it would not be noticed. She left the curtains open, so that the extra fullness could hang in front of the straight edge that held the letter. This done, she undressed and went to bed for a few hours. It was impossible; she lay with her eyes wide open, staring at the rectangle of the window, convinced a dark head and shoulders would appear. It was well past three when her eyes eventually fluttered shut. Not long after four, it happened.

Under normal sleeping circumstances, she might easily have missed it. It was not at all a loud noise, not loud enough to rouse other patrons of the establishment. There was a thumping sound from across the hall, in Harvey's room. She jumped out of bed, ran to her door and un-

locked it. The hall was dark. A single lamp burned low at
the far end, toward the stairs. No light issued from under
Harvey's door, but the thumping continued, louder now,
as she hesitantly approached its source. She took the door
handle and shook it, but the door was locked. Frightened
and uncertain how to proceed, she returned to her room for
a light. It was only half a minute later that she returned to
the hall, but already Carlisle's door stood open. She caught
a fleeting glimpse of a dark form running down the hall,
but her attention was mostly on Harvey, and the blood
streaming down his face.

"What happened? Come to my room at once. I'll awaken
Elleri and send for a doctor."

Carlisle looked as though he had single-handedly done
battle with a whole army. His eyes were puffed and one
was darkening. Blood streamed from his nose and the
corner of his mouth. His clothing, jacket and trousers,
were all disheveled. It was necessary for him to put an arm
around her shoulder to limp to her room.

She saw him to a chair before rousing her aunt. A
chattering, nervous lady was little enough help to either of
them. "Call a doctor, at once!" she demanded.

"No, we don't want to attract any attention to ourselves," Harvey said weakly.

"Did Kiley do this?" Vanessa asked, knowing the answer already.

"Yes. He did not believe my tale of an elopement, as
you warned from the start. He only pretended, to put me
off my guard. He got into my room while I slept. I cannot
imagine how he did it—I had the door locked. Oh, my
God! We'd better see if the letter is safe. I hope your
coming saved it, Vanessa. I had the valise pushed under
my bed, right against the wall. He may not have gotten to
it."

"Never mind that," she answered. "Auntie, bring the
basin of water and clean towels. We must send for help.
This left eye is cut."

"I have basilicum powder, gauze and plaster. I never
travel without them," she said, running back to her room
to get them.

Vanessa, looking at the bruised and bloodied young face before her, felt entirely culpable. She had brought this poor, innocent fellow to this state. She bathed the blood away gingerly, tenderly, asking at each stroke if it hurt.

"I don't know whether it is pain or ecstasy," he answered, looking into her eyes. It was hard to repress him, under the prevailing circumstances, so she ignored his meaningful words.

Elleri returned to add her noisy mite to the proceedings. Together the two women bathed his face, patched his various bruises and inveighed against the brutality of Kiley.

"But had we not better see about the letter?" Carlisle mentioned, more than once. "My door is not even locked . . ."

"We'd see him if he went in," Elleri pointed out.

Vanessa did not say the letter her case held was a hoax, but if he had his wits about him, she thought he must have guessed it. When he was feeling better, he rose up carefully, feeling his left shoulder with his right hand. "I'll go and see if he got it," he said.

"I'll go with you," Nessa said, looking around the room for a weapon. The poker stood by the grate. She took it up in one hand, lending her other to Harvey, who carried the lamp. While Miss Simons cleared away the medical supplies, the others went at a tardy, dragging gait to his room, leaving her and his doors open, to ensure a view of anyone trying to enter and steal the letter.

His chamber was a total shambles. The clothes-press door hung open, its contents tossed on the floor. Amidst the ruins, Vanessa saw her own belongings, petticoats and gowns, stockings and shawls, scattered hither and thither. Her suitcase was by the window, open and empty, with the lining torn up, the paper gone.

"He got it! Oh, Vanessa—what can I say? How can I *ever* make it up to you? I was supposed to be protecting it, and you, and now . . ."

"It's all right, Harvey. It's not your fault."

He looked at her, frowning. "You don't seem very upset."

"I *am* upset, that I put you through this, and very sorry too. Can you forgive me?"

"Forgive you? Forgive you for what, trusting a fool? But you did not trust me, did you? You knew how incompetent I was, how ill prepared to deal with a villain like Kiley. He is *vicious*. I never fought such an *animal* before, every manner of low trick. He learned his skills in an alley, kicking and punching my insides while I lay helpless in bed. If my organs aren't permanently injured, I will be much surprised. A gentleman would not . . . Well, we know what he is. But the letter—it is safe? I assume it was something else you hid under the lining, as you are taking this so calmly."

She set down the poker and began gathering up her apparel, tossing things at random into her case. She did not answer his question. He came up close behind her, turned her toward him and took her hands.

"I'm not offended at your not trusting me. As it turns out, you were the wiser of us. Your ruse fooled Kiley, and that is all that matters."

"No, it is not all that matters, Harvey. I am very sorry for what happened to you. It is my fault."

"Don't blame yourself. How should you have any idea of that man's brutality? You must let me help you. You see how dangerous he is. Only think if it were *you* he had attacked, rather than myself. A defenseless woman . . . It would make no difference to *him*, you know. Yes, it would, though. There are others, *worse* revenges he would take against a woman. You understand my meaning."

A shiver ran through her body. He put his arms around her, protectively. Suddenly his head came down, his lips looking for hers. The danger, the pity she felt for him, the flickering shadows the candle cast on the walls, the very nearness of a handsome and personable man—all had their effect. She allowed him to kiss her, and even found it rather pleasant, till she discovered how much stronger an effect it had on Harvey. He crushed her against him, beginning a much more passionate attack than she had anticipated.

"Oh, darling, my darling. You must let me protect you.

I can't bear to think of you at that man's mercy. Such innocence, such beauty and purity! Such . . ." He stopped whispering, and tried to kiss her again.

She tried to push him off, protesting. He held her more tightly, pressing his advances on her till she became quite frightened. "Harvey—stop! My aunt will be coming."

"Get rid of her. Send her back to bed, and return to me."

"Mr. Carlisle!" she gasped, aghast at the implications of his speech.

"Don't misunderstand! Oh, please, don't think *that* of me. I only meant we must make plans about delivering the letter safely. I know you will dislike to do it, but I think you should give it to me. Now that I am fully aware of Kiley's nature and convinced of his intentions, I will be much more careful. I want you out of all this awful business, my darling."

"That is kind of you, but really I am not at all sure you can handle Kiley any better than I can myself."

"I'll hire guards, or get hold of constables. This is too serious to allow of any further risk. Where is it?"

"It is hidden away safely."

"Yes, but where?"

"Where he won't find it. I *shall* call a constable, but not to accompany us. We must press charges against Kiley. Have the constable go after him. We cannot handle him alone."

"Your father wouldn't like it, to give so much publicity to it all. Secrecy surely is necessary."

"There will be no publicity involving me or the letter if *you* press charges against the man who beat you up and tried to rob you. The only ones who will make any connection between the two events are you, Kiley and myself. It will remove, or at least hamper, Kiley, and make my job easier."

"*Our* job," he corrected.

"You know you're not fit to travel. You could not possibly go on in this condition."

"Pshaw!" he said at once. "A black eye and a drawn cork aren't likely to stop me."

"What of the kicking, the beating, he administered while you were in bed?"

"I'll live. I *won't* let you go on unprotected. I'll see a doctor as soon as the message has been delivered."

She wanted only to pacify him and get away. "All right. All right, Harvey, I'll let you come, but only if you will lay charges this very night against Kiley. Why should we not? It will remove him from our affairs."

He considered a moment. "Very well. You are correct, as usual. I'll send an inn-boy off for the constable. Have him come here, for I will not leave you alone, at the mercy of that brute, for one single minute."

"Agreed," she said.

Miss Simons peered her head in at the door. "What chaos!" she exclaimed, looking all around the room.

"Kiley is demented," Harvey said, then he walked to his bell pull and gave it a few tugs. They waited at the door, with frequent darts across to Vanessa's room, till the messenger arrived.

"The constable won't want to come at this hour of the night," the boy pointed out.

"Bring him," Vanessa insisted. "Can't you see this man has been beaten within an inch of his life, and robbed?"

"What was took?" the boy asked.

The three exchanged a startled glance. Vanessa was the first to reach a decision. A man was more likely to be locked up if he had stolen something of considerable worth. "A hundred pounds, from Mr. Carlisle's purse," she said firmly.

Carlisle nodded. "A hundred pounds, slightly more, counting small bills and change."

The boy tilted his head in consideration, and apparently deemed the sum worth reporting to the constable in the middle of the night. He left to fetch him.

"My aunt and I will not want to be here when he comes," Vanessa said. "We want this to look like a simple robbery."

"Poor Harvey. The beating was not simple," Miss Simons said, shaking her head in sympathy.

"You two run along. I'll speak to the constable, then go

to you. It will be daylight by then. You will want an early start, I should think?''

"Yes, come to us as soon as he leaves," Vanessa said.

They went first to Vanessa's room, to talk together a few moments. ''Why don't you try to get a little more sleep?'' the niece suggested. ''We'll have to be up early enough.''

Yawning, her aunt agreed, with only the addendum that she knew she could not possibly sleep, but she would just lie down and rest awhile. Within minutes, soft, gurgling snores were coming through the open door. Vanessa went quietly forward and closed the door. She looked at her aunt's traveling clock on the dresser, wondering which would come first, Carlisle or the inn servant with her masquerade suit. If it chanced to be Harvey, she would have to stave him off with some excuse till she had changed and left. It would be better to be wearing a dress, so she changed into street clothes, thinking that with her luck, the two of them would arrive at her door together, to reveal her plan. Once or twice she went to the door, put her ear to it and listened for sounds in the hall, but heard nothing. The constable was taking his time about answering the call. In the end, she decided to try for a little rest. She would just lie on top of the counterpane in her gown till one or the other of the expected knocks sounded.

Before doing this, she walked in the darkness, her candle extinguished now, to the window, planning to look out and ensure no one was loitering on the balcony. She must also check the curtain hem, to see the letter was still safe. There was no movement and no sound in the blackness beyond her window. She felt the lock at the window's top, then gasped in shock. It was undone! Someone had unfastened the latch from the inside. The glass was not broken. While she and her aunt had been out, someone had sneaked in and undone the latch, planning to slip in after she was asleep. What other explanation could there be? Her fingers trembled, her whole body shook, as she slid the bolt back into place. Kiley! It was Kiley who had been in her room, at some point during those visits to and fro between Harvey's room and her own. How did he have the gall to do it, right under her nose? He was part cat, to move so stealthily, with no one hearing or seeing him.

The letter! Had he got it? She looked down at the hem. It was very dark, too dark to be certain the curtain bulged at a suspicious angle. It could be only shadows. She was not certain those darker spots beneath the curtain were boots either, though they looked dreadfully like it. "Please, God, make them be shadows," she said under her breath.

CHAPTER
Twelve

SHE STOOD, HER breath suspended with fright, staring at the dark spots beneath the curtain. When the spots moved ever so little, she jumped back as though on a string, with no consciousness that she did it. There was a blur of swaying drapery, then a large pair of shoulders moved in the faint light from the window, moved swiftly to place themselves behind her. A hand was clamped over her mouth; the other arm went around her waist, pulling her firmly back against a man's chest. He had been there all the time, hiding behind the curtain, to attack her. He had even watched her change her clothing. She was nearly as angry as she was frightened, but with a sudden, vivid memory of Harvey's bloody face and bruised body and his ominous warning of what fate Kiley might visit on a woman, fear soon overtook all other emotions. She thought her heart would stop, as she stood, locked against him. There was not a sound in the room but his rapid breathing and her own, till a particularly loud snore erupted through Elleri's adjoining door, to tell her how much help her aunt was likely to be in her hour of dire need.

"Don't make a sound. I have a gun," Kiley said softly in her ear. "I'm not going to hurt you. I just want the letter. Where is it?"

No answer was possible, with his fingers crushing her lips. He removed them, no more than an inch, ready to clamp back in place if she started to scream. She was too dazed, too frightened, to do so. She gulped the air, trembling.

"Light a candle," he ordered, still holding her against him. "We'll walk to your bed table. You light it. You'll feel my gun in your back, in case you get any unladylike ideas."

She did exactly as he commanded, still too frightened to make any rational plan, but a rag of hope at least fluttered. He didn't have the letter! He hadn't found it, though he had been standing right beside it. Her shaking fingers fumbled in the darkness, taking a long time to strike the flint and get a faint, flickering light. She was so shaken, she sat on the side of the bed to look at the enemy. Menacing shadows danced over his face, while his black eyes examined her. In his right hand, a lethal pistol pointed at her heart. Behind him on the wall, his shadow rose up to the ceiling, as menacing as all the rest.

"Sorry if I frightened you," he said, "but this is too serious a matter to allow sentiment to intrude. I want the letter. I will have it before I leave this room. Many lives are at stake. It is amply clear to me by now that you will not succeed in delivering it safely. Your friend Carlisle has called in reinforcements. I was attacked on the road coming from Maldon, barely escaping with my life. The same carriage arrived at the stables here not an hour ago. Whatever his personal feelings, he won't go on treating you with kid gloves once his cohorts get to persuading him."

She continued looking at him, mute. She could not have spoken if she wanted to. She was paralyzed with fear and shock.

"Come, now, you have nothing to fear. When I go and you remain, they'll know I have it, and be chasing off after me. I am better able to handle their sort. Two ladies have no chance against them. Where is it?"

She licked her lips. "I don't have it," she said, her voice a mere whisper.

"I repeat, where is it?" he asked, his voice becoming harsher.

"I gave it to Carlisle."

He shook his head. "Try again. I went through his room and case with a fine tooth comb. I fancy you played him the same stunt you played me. I assume you had one of your blank calling cards pasted under the lining of your valise. He would not still be hanging around if it had been the real letter. You've still got it." His eyes made a tour of the room, then settled on her body, appraising it as he had when first they met. "I believe on your person is the likeliest place."

"Did you see it when you watched me undress?"

"No," he answered quietly, with a little flush. "Your back was to me the whole time. I didn't see anything . . . I mean . . ." He quickly caught himself up, becoming hard, insistent again. "Hand it over, or I will be forced to take it. If I have to strip you naked, Miss Bradford, I will do it. Make no mistake about that."

"Please, I don't have it."

"Take off your dress," he said in a completely impersonal but very firm tone.

She looked, clutching at her bosom. She slowly arose and began backing away, toward her aunt's door, hoping against hope to arouse her. He raised the gun, cocked it, the metallic click sounding like thunder in the closed room. "Back this way, to the bed—away from the door," he ordered. When she remained motionless, he took her arm and pulled her back roughly.

"I don't like this any more than you do. A great deal of unpleasantness and time can be spared if you'll just hand it over. I will deliver it for you. For God's sake, give it to me, Vanessa!" he said, his voice rising louder than before. "I don't want to do anything we'll both regret."

She swallowed convulsively, and inched back. His hand flew out and grabbed her, pushing her against the wall. "You bring it on yourself," he charged angrily, then reached out and grabbed the top of her gown, gave a wrench that ripped it open to the waist, revealing her camisole. With only a second's hesitation, his fingers closed over the top of this. A ring on his second finger scratched against her soft flesh, while every finger pressed hard against her bosom.

"Sure you don't want to change your mind?" he asked, examining her closely. His eyes slid from her face down to her half-exposed breasts, which rose and fell from her turbulent breathing. His own breaths were quick and shallow. There was a nervous, febrile quality in him that had not been there before. Without any experience in such matters, she knew it was caused by those fingers, twitching against her white breasts. He seemed fascinated by them, making it easy to believe Harvey's warning of the revenge awaiting a woman at this man's hands. "Well?" he asked, tightening his hold, ready to rip away the last covering.

"Wait. I'll get it," she said.

"Good girl." A smile flickered quickly over his features. He looked for a moment, then his head swept down and he kissed her—only a fleeting kiss, but full on the lips. He lifted his head reluctantly. "Danger is the greatest aphrodisiac in the world. Did you know that?" he asked.

"What?"

"And you, undressed, run it a very close second."

She held her breath while he slowly uncurled his fingers from her camisole, to let them slide over her breasts, taking more time than was necessary to do it. At last he took a step backward, no longer touching her with anything but his eyes.

She looked around the room, searching for a weapon. She had left her poker in Harvey's room. Nothing else looked large enough or strong enough to disable him, even temporarily. Then she saw Elleri's traveling clock, its brass frame holding the glass that protected the works within. Its sharp corners were suitable for her purpose. She took a quick step past him; he was after her, reaching for her arm.

"It's there, in the clock," she said. He came along with her, still holding onto her, still with the pistol in his left hand, but hanging down by his side now. She reached for the clock—he held her hand away from it, with a look more arch than anything else.

"You wouldn't fool a fellow, would you? Funny the clock is still running," he mentioned, looking at her suspiciously.

"I folded the letter up tight. It's behind the brass backing. It will have to be unscrewed. Do you have anything . . ."

"My clasp knife should do it," he said. He let go of her for a moment while he reached into his inner jacket pocket, having a little difficulty to extract the knife with one hand. She picked the clock up, not swiftly, to reveal her plan, but in a casual way that did not alarm him. Then, while his head was turned down toward the pocket, she swiftly raised the clock and brought its square corner down hard against his temple. He fell to the floor with a little groan. She didn't know whether she had killed or only wounded him, and didn't care much at that instant. At least he was immobile. She ran to the curtain, extracted the letter, threw on her bonnet and pelisse to cover her rent gown, picked up her reticule and dashed out the door, without telling her aunt or anyone. She wanted only to escape, to run while she had the chance, to take the letter and not stop running till it was safely delivered. There was no time for a masculine disguise, or a groom to protect her. There was only the blind panic that said "escape."

She went downstairs to the lobby, where the staff was just beginning preparations for the morning. In the short interval she had been with Kiley, the sun had risen. "When does the first coach leave?" she asked the clerk.

"At six-thirty, ma'am. You have plenty of time. You can grab a bite of breakfast first, if you like. The coffee will be ready presently."

"Thank you. I can't wait." She ran out the door into the street. It was cool in the first light of morning, and practically deserted. There was a man driving a milk cart toward the inn, and a man going into a shop, stopping to unlock the door, obviously the proprietor. She had not thought to ask the clerk which direction the coach stop lay.

She ran across the street to enquire this information of the shopkeeper. As she hastened along, she caught the loose toe of her shoe on a cobblestone, pulling it loose, right back to the heel. It flapped, hampering her progress, lending a grotesque air to her fleeing steps.

"Can you direct me to the coach stop?" she asked.

He looked at her pale, harried young face and took pity on her. "Yes, miss, it's two blocks down the street, on your right. Are you in some trouble?"

"No, just in a hurry," she answered.

"There's no rush. You've three-quarters of an hour yet."

"Thank you." She glanced up to see what manner of a shop he had, wondering if it were not safer than a coaching house. When Kiley came to and found her gone, he would check first the stable at the inn, then the coaching stop.

"Would you like to come in and wait?" he offered. It was a drapery shop. "I usually make myself a pot of tea before the customers come in."

The shop was across from the inn, giving her a good view of comings and goings there. She could see if Kiley came out, without being seen by him. A drapery shop too would have needle and thread to repair her torn gown. "Thank you," she said, and took a step toward him. He noticed her shuffling walk, and soon saw its cause.

"I can fix that for you. I have a hammer and some tacks out back. I use them for small repairs about the shop. It will take care of you till you can get to a proper cobbler. I don't have a last, but we'll stick a bit of metal into the shoe. I hope the tacks don't go through the insole to pierce your toes. You can always put some cardboard inside your shoe if the tacks come through." He chattered on in this amiable fashion while they went inside. Although it was quite dark, he did not light candles. In fact, he bolted the door behind them, explaining that he was not actually open for business yet. This gave her some feeling of security.

"Thank you. You are very helpful," she said.

"I'll just light my little fire and set the water boiling for tea. Then I'll fix your shoe for you."

She thought for a moment, then said, "Why don't you bring me the hammer and tacks, and I'll tack it while you start the fire?"

"Do you know how to use a hammer?" he asked, laughing. He seemed a nice fatherly gentleman.

"I'll manage. What am I to use for a last?"

He poked around behind his counters and came up with a flat piece of sheet metal, which he inserted for her. It was not the right shape, but was better than nothing. He heard the slow, tentative tapping while he made his fire, smiled to himself at the unlikely picture of an elegant young lady turning cobbler. He also wondered what scrape she had fallen into, but in the end decided it was none of his business. If he started asking questions, he would only end up having to give her money. Poverty did not appear to be her problem, though.

Vanessa stationed herself at the counter for her chore, with a clear view of the inn. There was a little traffic, but neither Kiley, Carlisle nor her aunt came out. The kettle was humming by the time she finished her job. There was no time to find needle and thread; already the cups were rattling. She hastily grabbed up a few loose pins from the counter and pinned her torn gown, in a temporary way, then pulled her pelisse over her shoulders, to conceal the rough job.

The draper smiled at the mess she had done of repairing her shoe—it looked lumpy, amateurish. She had got the sole pulled crooked, poor thing. They drank their tea while she quizzed him about coaches, and especially their destinations.

"The first to leave is the day stage to London. It's slow—the public stage, stops everywhere. It would get you in around four this afternoon. Is it London you're off to?"

"Yes," she answered, sticking to her decision to follow that route, in hopes of fooling Kiley.

She checked out the window, across the road to the inn, before leaving the drapery shop. "It's a bit early yet," the man pointed out.

"I want to be sure to get a seat. Thank you so very much."

"You're entirely welcome, my dear."

He shook his head, to see her pelt down the street as if the hounds of hell were after. Running away, he figured, and no more able to take care of herself than a baby. But what she lacked in experience she made up in determination. She would have a seat on that stage if she had to sit on the box with the driver, wearing a man's drab coat and hat. The situation was not quite so desperate. There was a seat inside. She read the posted schedule, disliking that it was such a slow stage, stopping at every hamlet. So much chance for mischief, for being overtaken. The mail coach would be definitely better, faster, but unfortunately it did not arrive for some hours, and her first priority was to get away from Colchester.

While she stood worrying, an elegant old dame strode up beside her and stopped, arms akimbo as she looked all around. She had gray hair, a good but ancient black outfit and a hatchet nose that lent an air of breeding to her. "Where *is* that wretched boy?" the dame asked, of no one in particular. "I shall never take my grandson up in my carriage again." She turned to Vanessa, to have someone to complain to. "He must be forever running off to the stables to talk to the grooms. I declare we shan't be to London before noon."

As she spoke, an elegant black carriage harnessed up to a team of four was led out. "Only look at the wretched job horses they have saddled me with," the woman jawed, but the team were deep-chested bays, capable of a good speed. Vanessa glanced over to the day stage, to compare. But there was no comparison; even without all the necessary stops, the stage could never keep pace with this rig. Besides the groom, there was a man mounted behind for protection. A little boy of six or seven came darting up to the woman.

"Come along, dear," she said impatiently. "Always the same," she added aside to Vanessa. "Traveling is a dead bore. I shan't leave my home again if I can avoid it. I would not be going to London now, but my grandson is going to visit his cousins there. They are taking him to Brighton for a holiday, eh, Bobbie?''

"I am going to go sailing in the sea," the boy announced proudly. He was a bright-eyed boy, but with a pallor that suggested the reason for the holiday was therapeutic.

"Traveling by the stage is much worse," Vanessa said, pinning a pitiful smile on her face.

"The stage! Good gracious, you never mean a lady like yourself is traveling by the common stage! I made sure you were awaiting your carriage. And unchaperoned too," she added in deep disgust.

Vanessa feared this solecism was going to rob her of a seat in the woman's carriage, which she had set her mind on as vastly preferable to the stage. The sprightly bays' harnesses jingled as they chomped at the ground, eager to be off. And the carriage half empty! She took her courage in her hands to talk herself into an invitation. "It is a case of the greatest urgency," she began. "My father brought me from Chelmsford, where I was to be met, but the carriage did not come for me. I cannot imagine what happened to it. It must have met with an accident, I suppose. I have never been on a stage before. I hope it is not too horrid."

The woman hesitated a moment before answering. At length she asked, "Where are you going, my dear?"

The question was hardly necessary. The customers present were all going to London; that was the only stage leaving at that time. "To London, ma'am."

"Why, you must come with me. I shall be happy for the company. This sad rattle of a fellow will be nodding before we have gone a mile. Small wonder too," she added. "He was up till midnight. A very noisy inn we stayed at, the Three Cups. I did not like it above half."

With a sigh of joy, Vanessa climbed into the carriage, behind the dame, before her grandson. "Where are you bound for in London?" the hostess asked. "But first, we must exchange names. It would not do to share a carriage with a total stranger," she added, in accents rather similar to Miss Simons. "My name is Mrs. Euston." She glanced to her new companion for an appreciation of this fact.

"I am Vanessa Bradford," she answered, without a single fear in the world now. She had her protection. She mentally selected a relative in London, for she must actually go to one after delivering her message. "I am going to stay with my aunt, Mrs. Halford."

"I see. Where does she live?"

"In Belgrave Square."

"You never mean it!" the woman exclaimed, her eyes widening in delight.

"Why, do you know her?"

"Know her—my dear, we shall be neighbors. I am taking Bobbie to Belgrave Square, to the Winterses' home. My daughter married Sir Horace Winters, the magistrate. They live in that fine old brick mansion just at the top of the loop. A great drafty place in winter, but it will do well enough in this weather. I fully expect we shall be parboiled with the heat before we get there. Where did you say you were from, Miss Bradford?"

"I live near Hastings."

"You would not be Colonel Bradford's girl?"

"*I* am a general!" Bobbie informed them.

"Yesterday he was an admiral. I believe I have met your papa. My late husband was with the Foreign Office. We knew many of the military. Very likely I have met him, though I cannot attach a face to the name."

"Papa is tall and dark—he was in India for some time. His hair is gray now." A vivid picture of her father reared up in her head. She was proud and happy that she was at last accomplishing the job he had given her.

"We knew *all* the Indian military. Of course I know him. I remember him very well now. He was used to tease Bertie, my late husband, about something or other. Some orders your papa sent to England that were never filled, or not to his satisfaction, at any rate."

This sounded very like her father, to be dissatisfied with officialdom. She could hardly credit her luck in falling in with a friend so felicitously. "So you are going to visit the Halfords." Mrs. Euston smiled happily. Then her grandson began wetting his finger and drawing on the window glass, which brought their conversation to a halt while he was reprimanded. Far from dozing off, the boy was a positive plague throughout the trip, scrambling over their feet every time a carriage or even a dray horse was passed on the road. Intermittent conversation had to be kept up for appearance's sake, for Mrs. Euston was fond of talk.

Vanessa bore these petty annoyances with goodwill, knowing circumstances would have been worse on the stage and would have endured for more hours. It was a relief when Mrs. Euston said, "We shall have to stop for a change of team soon."

The relief soon turned to consternation. Public stops were seen as jeopardous. The woman's next statement was pure delight. "I have cousins a few miles along the road. I change there, usually. Arrangements have been made for me to do so on this trip. It is very convenient having friends and relatives sprinkled about the countryside. Not so convenient when *they* are passing by my home, and making use of my facilities, but there, they scratch my back and I scratch theirs."

"My back is itchy," Bobbie said. "Are we going to stop at Uncle Euston's?"

"Certainly we are, and you must not get dirty in the stable."

Soon the coachman turned off the main road, to drive the carriage down a smaller road, a lane really, with scarcely room to pass. "I cannot imagine why Reginald does not widen this sheep path," Mrs. Euston scolded. "He should have some thought to his visitors' carriages, if he don't care for his own. We'll be fortunate if we don't lose a wheel."

When they approached the house, no more than a thatched cottage, Vanessa rather wondered that Reginald could afford to have a road at all, and not that he did not improve it. They were let down at the front door.

"Take the carriage to the stable and hitch up the new team at once, Bottom," she commanded. "We shall take a cup of tea, but nothing more. We do not want to waste a whole hour here. A little rest will not go amiss, however.

You and Barnes take only one glass of ale, mind. We don't want you tipsy.'' Then she turned to Vanessa, saying, "I should have got my netting out of the carriage. Is there anything you require?'' She stopped suddenly, frowning. "Why, we never packed your trunk! We left it at the coaching house. Fancy neither of us thinking of it.''

Vanessa's mouth flew open in guilty dismay. "I—I *did* leave my trunk on the coach,'' she said, "but it is no matter. There is nothing of any importance in it. Only my clothing. My aunt will have it picked up for me in London.''

"The stage stops at Stephen's Hotel, on Bond Street, if I am not mistaken?''

"Yes,'' Vanessa answered, quite at random, for she had not determined this point in her reading of the schedule.

"What time does it arrive?''

"At four. I can easily do without my things till then,'' she said airily. They proceeded up the walk to a rickety stoop and dilapidated door.

"Mercy, how some folks live,'' Mrs. Euston complained. "One would never guess to look at this hovel that Reginald Euston has the better part of two hundred thousand in the funds. Skint. He is my late husband's brother, a retired naval man, but you must not be surprised if he looks more like a clod-crusher. He has let himself go.'' This inconsequential chatter continued till they were admitted to the house by a slatternly maid wearing a dirty apron and unkempt hair.

"I am Mrs. Euston. Reginald knows I am stopping to change my team,'' she said. "Is he here?''

"He's at the stable, mum. I didn't know you was coming, but he'll see by your carriage you've got here.''

"Slattern,'' Mrs. Euston said, looking after her. "Reginald's wife is dead, which accounts for the state of this place.'' She drew out a handkerchief to dust off the chair before sitting down with a grunt. "Where is Bobbie? The rascal darted straight off to the stable again. He'll come in filthy. Maybe I should go after him. No, I won't, though. I'll send the girl for him when she brings tea.''

She looked around the dingy parlor, disapproval on every line and wrinkle of her raddled old face. She regaled

Vanessa with some of Reginald's naval exploits, till the tea was brought in. She sent the girl off for Bobbie, poured tea and said, "Do you take anything in it?"

"A little milk, please, no sugar."

"You are not wise. The milk is curdling. There, I shall put in a little sugar to hide the wretched taste." She passed the cup along. "I don't believe I shall have any milk," she said, then she sipped judiciously. "This is cheap tea, ground-up stems. I doubt there was a leaf in the lot. It tastes bitter, does it not?"

"It is not bohea, Mrs. Euston, but I am thirsty from the drive," Vanessa said, drinking thirstily.

"I shall send the slattern for fresh milk. It is the curdled milk that is destroying the taste. I am fussy about my tea."

"It's not bad," Vanessa replied, her wish being to drink it up quickly, say thank you to Reginald Euston and get back on the road. She took another sip, then felt queasy. She put the cup down, leaned back against the chair and closed her eyes.

"Gracious, I hope you are not going to be ill!" Mrs. Euston exclaimed.

"No. I did not take any breakfast. I'm feeling faint, that's all."

"I'll order some bread and butter."

"Please—don't . . ." She felt a wave of nausea, opened her eyes, shook her head and looked for the closest door. It seemed a great distance away, though she had not taken ten steps from it to her chair. While she still looked, a strange phenomenon occurred. The room turned into a long, dark tunnel, the door a diminutive hole at its farthest end. Mr. Carlisle, with one eye swollen and blackened, staring at her, was the last thing she was conscious of before the tunnel began swaying, then closed in over her head, as she slumped from the chair.

CHAPTER
Thirteen

WHEN VANESSA REGAINED consciousness, she lay
on a foul-smelling bed in a small room, with her hands
tied behind her back. It was still daylight, the only satis-
factory feature of her surroundings. Darkness would have
been worse. Her head did not ache; it felt hollow, or
stuffed with cotton wool. A strange lethargy invaded her
whole being, a feeling that things did not matter, because
they were unreal. It was very odd to be in a strange and
dirty room—what could account for it? The blanket thrown
over her was rough against her skin. As she stretched her
stiff fingers against her lower spine, she realized she was not
wearing any clothing. This, like the other bizarre aspects of
her condition, she found mildly curious. For several minutes
she lay awake, yet not entirely alert, looking at a series of
brown watermarks on the wall. They seemed strangely
familiar to her. Oh, yes, she thought with a smile, the Outer
Hebrides—a large, wider mark on top, dwindling to narrower
and shorter ones in the south, the whole group slightly
curved. This recognition offered some sense of security.
She knew now where she was, at the Outer Hebrides.

As she became more fully awake, she realized her arms were uncomfortably stiff. By wriggling her wrists and hands, the ropes that bound her were shrugged off without too much difficulty. Her jailer had done a careless job. He had been in a hurry, or she was considered harmless due to her condition. She sat up, holding the blanket to her chin with one hand, the rope in the other, for examination. The past events began, slowly, to seep back into her mind, bringing a sense of dread. Mr. Carlisle at the parlor door, looking at her, not with the adoring face of yore, but with a quite different expression. Vicious was the word that came to mind. She felt a shiver along her spine, soon followed by a terrible apprehension for her safety, her very life. She would never be allowed to go free, now that she knew him for what he was. Her only chance for survival was to escape, before they knew she had regained consciousness.

The letter was her next thought. Had they got it? She jumped out of bed, wrapping the blanket around her. Her clothing was gone, every stitch of it carried away. She tried the door, being careful to make little noise, and found it locked. The only furnishing other than the bed was a small chest of drawers. Hoping to find some clothing, she walked silently to it, eased open the four drawers, one after the other, to find it contained four ancient hats, one moth-eaten gentleman's beaver and three ladies' bonnets, covered in wilting flowers and faded feathers. There was no carpet on the floor, no canopy on the bed, no draperies at the windows, no possible hiding place, and nothing to manufacture clothing. She ran to the window to examine her chances for escape by that means. She was on a second story, looking down a sheer wall to a patch of hard-packed earth, with not even a blade of grass to cushion her drop.

A jump would not kill her, but it would quite possibly break a leg, making escape impossible. It was clear why they had been careless of her bindings; she was as helpless as if she were in chains, locked in a room with no clothing and no means of escape. If she used the blanket as a rope to help her descend, she would have to enter the outdoors stark naked. And really the blanket, a thick woolen thing, was not at all capable of being tied into knots, nor was there anything near the window to tether it to. Was she to sit like a rat in a trap, waiting for them to come and—what? Kill her? Assault, molest her? Yes, Carlisle's expression had been violent enough that he would exact every revenge before killing her.

Worst of all, they had found the letter, they *must* have found it. They had taken all her things. Maybe they had gone away, abandoned her in their haste to deliver the news to their superiors. She wanted to go to the door and rattle it, yell and scream and see if there was anyone in the house. Yet if there *was* someone . . . If, say, Carlisle, was lurking about downstairs waiting for her to revive . . . No, she would wait and think and try to devise a plan of self-rescue. Her efforts were hampered by the awful panic rising in her bosom. Her whole body trembled; she felt ill, whether from the drugged tea or fear, she did not know, nor did it matter. She crouched on the end of the bed, trying to calm her nerves, to strengthen her resolve. Her throat was dry and painful, so painful as to be an added distraction.

How had she got here? Carlisle, obviously, had arranged it. He had been her enemy from the start, then. Kiley was right. He had followed her, perhaps all the way from Hastings, had discovered at the inn at Tilbury that she was going to Raffertys, and gone after her. He either actually knew Edward Rafferty or discovered that a son existed, and something of his interests and whereabouts—enough to hazard an appearance at the door. She reviewed all his seeming innocence and naiveté, his accepting her story that she carried diamonds, his kind offer first to accompany her, then his gradual insinuation into her confidence, his request to be given the letter to "protect." And all the time he was luring her along to this—to get her alone and take the letter by force. The reinforcements Kiley had spoken of at Colchester must have been Mrs. Euston and the men on the carriage with her. Mrs. Euston, so conveniently going to London with an empty carriage, when she saw herself reading the London schedule. Had she said she was going to Ipswich, the empty carriage would have been headed in that direction. Bobbie's part in it was unclear, but she took him for a real grandson, used to add an air of naturalness to the woman's appearance. Who would suspect a grandmother and child of such treachery?

And what about Kiley? He was not who he said either. Had he come from her father, he would have had some proof. He would have known her destination without learning it from Carlisle. Most damning of all, he would not have opened the letter to Sir Giles. He would have delivered it. He was some separate spy; no doubt Napoleon had dozens of them working independently. She could not account for the animosity of the two men, unless they were professional competitors, both spies, both after her letter, but not working together. This being the case, she was surprised it was Carlisle who had won out. She would have put her faith in Kiley for being the more clever and ruthless of the two.

Her thoughts were interrupted by the clattering of a horse and carriage rolling up in front of the house. She could not see it, but she heard the sounds. Soon she heard faint stirrings belowstairs, knocks and bumps and an occasional grunt loud enough to rise up through the floor. The commotion, fight, from the sounds of it, was going on in the room immediately below her. Another falling out among the thieves, probably about the letter or herself. She had the ominous sensation that the victor would bolt up the stairs, unlock the door and confront her, quite possibly rape her—and what could she do to stop him? She could jump out the window naked or she could wait. She looked to the window, knowing there was a carriage out front. A person could hide her nakedness in a carriage.

The decision was taken from her. Within a split second of the thought, there was a hard pounding on the stairs, steps hurrying down the hall. The door rattled. He was here!

''Miss Bradford! Vanessa—are you all right?'' She recognized Kiley's voice, though it was strained, tense and unnatural-sounding.

She swallowed, looked fruitlessly around the room, knowing there was no place to hide. She got up off the bed, pulling the blanket about her, silent with dread. The door was suddenly heaving, as it was subjected to kicks, or possibly a straining shoulder. There was the sound of shattering wood, and suddenly he was there, panting, gasping, staring at her. She stared back; neither of them said a word.

When he had recovered his breath, Kiley said, "Are you all right?" He sounded remarkably angry.

She went on looking at him, her throat too dry and sore to answer, but her eyes conveying her fear and loathing. "Are you all right?" he asked, more loudly, more angrily. "For God's sake *say* something! What did they do to you?"

"They got the letter," she said.

He took three long strides to her. "How did they get it? What did they do?"

"I don't know. I was drugged."

"They left you like this, naked?" His eyes ran around the room, saw the rope on the bed. "Were you beaten, abused in any way? Raped?"

"No, I don't have any scars or pain. Carlisle is not so vicious as you, Kiley." She was past caring what she said. Her shoulders slumped in defeat.

"I should have killed the bastard while I had the chance. Get dressed. We're leaving."

"I don't have any clothes. They took them."

"Look around the other rooms. There must be something you can put on. I have to see the man I knocked out downstairs isn't planning any mischief. There was a serving wench ran out to the stable. She may have gone for help. I'll tie the man up and come back to you. We must hurry."

He left, turned and walked out, leaving the door unlocked. She went into the hallway, entered the next room, a man's, to judge from the shirts and trousers on the bed. Across the hall was a female's chamber, in a great state of disarray. A part of the mess was her own gown and underclothing. She looked for her shoes but did not see them. The gown, already ripped to the waist, had been completely destroyed, pulled in three pieces. Was it spite, or did they think she had in some manner concealed the letter in its folds or seams? The flounce, a double flounce, had been pulled completely off the gown, to lay in a puddle on the floor. She quickly put on her underclothing, happy to get out of the scratchy blanket, then went to the clothes press to see what gowns hung there.

They were all large, dark and unfashionable—gowns that suited and probably belonged to Mrs. Euston. She took one from the hanger, her nose wrinkling in disgust at its moldering condition. Before she had time to slip it over her head, Kiley was back. That he should unceremoniously walk in while she wore only her petticoats was not remarkable, after the greater indignities she had suffered. She directed one brief glance at him, then put the gown over her head.

"I tied him up. The wench is gone," Kiley said. "Do you need a hand?"

As she was about to decline his offer, she noticed the gown hooked up the back. She turned around, still not speaking, but letting him discover for himself what was to be done. His fingers flew along, skipping every second hook.

"They've gone toward London," he said.

"Who?"

"Carlisle and the woman, and those men that were on the carriage."

"How do you know?"

"A little boy out front told me. A child, too young to have learned to lie yet, I think. I would have met them if they'd gone the other way. They weren't met on the road from Colchester. I kept a sharp eye out."

"You're going after them?" she asked.

"We're going after them."

"You don't need me. Let me go back to my aunt."

"By what means? You don't have a carriage. I promised your father I would look after you. I have done a damned poor job of it thus far, haven't I? I can't leave you here alone, and I can't spare the time to take you." His hands jerked roughly on the hooks.

She turned to look at him, frowning, trying to figure out his part in her escapade. "Don't look at me like that," he said. "It's not *all* my fault. If you'd done as I asked in the first place, none of this would have happened. Not to *you*, at least."

His harsh features, which she was accustomed to see set in lines of determination and anger, were softened to regret. His eyes too bore traces of sympathy, perhaps pity. "Was it very bad?" he asked, his tone gentle.

"No, not so very bad. I was drugged as soon as I arrived. The trip was not unpleasant."

"Was Carlisle in the carriage?"

"No, I caught a glimpse of him at the parlor door, just as I passed out from the tea. They put something in it, in my cup."

"It was the big gray-haired woman calling herself Mrs. Euston who brought you? I saw her talking to Carlisle at the inn."

"Yes, her and the boy. He was her grandson, she said. She even knew my aunt, which made me feel secure . . ."

"Claimed to know her, after she wormed a name and probably an address out of you."

"It might have been that way. Yes, I think I told her."

"How did she lure you to this isolated spot?"

"By stopping at her relative's place to change teams. It all seemed so natural, the way she scolded and—everything."

"She's a pro, probably been doing this sort of thing for years."

"But who is she?"

"An accomplice of Carlisle's. Possibly some relative—I really have no idea."

"They're not French. Why should they be helping Napoleon?"

"For money. That's all—the job pays well. *French* spies working for France are patriots, as English ones working for England are. It is the turncoats that are despicable. Even their employers despise them. Still, they'll be paid handsomely for their information, and that's all they're

interested in. They cannot have much of a head start on us.
Let's go.''

She turned around, trying to decide on Kiley's innocence. ''Mr. Kiley,'' she began.

''My name is Landon, remember? Colonel Landon. You
cannot know how I have come to detest the name of
Kiley.''

''Did my father really send you?''

''How else should I have got here?''

''How did Carlisle? Spies have ways . . .''

''Well, you know, Miss Bradford, it is very much your
own fault that Carlisle is here. Yours and your father's. I
do not feel he acted at all wisely either in sending his
message with a pair of ladies.''

''I didn't tell anyone.''

''You and your aunt stopped to examine the preparations for the ball at Hastings before leaving. Your father
told you to go *directly* to Sir Giles Harkman. If you had
followed his orders, no one would have followed you in time
to be of any danger. A great deal of curiosity was gener-
ated at learning of the sudden trip, and at such an unlikely
time. That, coupled with your father's known great interest
in Napoleon's preparations, was bound to lead any wide-
awake fellow, which I think we must grant Carlisle to be,
to suspect there was more to the voyage than a visit to a
friend.''

''I didn't believe the message had any importance. I
thought Papa was just being mean. He doesn't like me to
have much to do with the officers at home. If you really
came from him, why did you not bring any proof?''

''He was not at all eager for me to go after you, at first,
anyway. He thought it would draw attention to you, till I
mentioned I had my civilian clothing with me. When I
learned the sort of talk running around the garrison, I knew
I must leave. I changed into mufti, and only stopped a
moment to tell him I was going. In our consternation, we
neither of us thought of a letter of introduction. And when
I was told at Tilbury that you had already been attacked, I
knew I was right to have gone after you. I *don't* understand how you trusted Carlisle so implicitly, and myself

not at all. What did he do, what charm did he work, to convince you?''

''I did not trust him completely. It is only that he chanced along at Raffertys in such an innocent-seeming manner . . .''

''We'll talk in the curricle. Come on.''

''I don't have any shoes,'' she said, lifting up the long, loose-hanging gown to display her bare toes.

''They even took your shoes?'' he asked.

''Yes,'' she said with a worried look, wondering whether to tell him all. He regarded her fixedly.

For a moment, there was some consciousness of constraint between them. ''I see,'' he said, in a meaningful voice. ''When you have come to trust me completely, you will of course tell me why *that* disturbs you, when the gown's being destroyed does not. If you had the letter in your shoe, I don't see why they would not just pull it out and leave the shoes behind. Maybe they did. Let's have a look.''

They both began looking around the room, but Vanessa went to the clothes press for a pair of Mrs. Euston's shoes. She knew her own were gone, their secret discovered.

''Ha, just as I said. Here they are,'' Landon exclaimed, pulling one out from under the bed. Its toe just protruded from the covers. ''The other must be here somewhere,'' he said, handing the one up to her. She looked, to determine it was the innocent one she held.

''The other won't be there,'' she said flatly.

''Wrong. Here it is,'' he announced triumphantly, reaching a long arm far under the bed to retrieve it.

She gave a gasp of surprise and reached for it, staring to see if the sole had been torn loose. It had not. Somehow, in their haste and probably because they thought her too stupid to invent a good hiding place, they had tossed it aside. Landon too stared at the shoe, not passing it to her, but looking at it with a curious smile on his lips.

''I believe I underestimated you, Vanessa,'' he said, ripping the sole back, while her carefully hammered tacks sprang out, revealing the well-worn, folded letter. A glowing smile alit on his face. He put his head back and laughed loud. "By God, and here I thought you had it in the top of your stocking! I knew it wasn't in your bodice at any rate. I *do* apologize for having to confirm it." He unfolded the letter as he spoke.

She reached for it, while he pulled back. "Oh, no, this time *I* keep it."

She was possessed by a strong desire to get it back, but as that was unlikely, she had to determine that Landon was absolutely to be trusted. There had to be some way she could discover it.

"What's the matter?" he asked, still smiling. "Have I not absolved myself yet?"

"Of course," she prevaricated, sensing that a genial approach would be her best chance of success. "I am just worried—about my father, along with all the rest. He was not well when I left, you know, which is why he sent me. How did he seem when you spoke to him?"

"Not in very high gig, as a matter of fact, but not dangerously ill. Parkins, his batman, was tending him, and sending for the sawbones."

"Was he in bed?"

"No, but in his bedchamber, sitting at that great campaign desk he took as booty in the Netherlands. A handsome piece. He was taking Irish tea, and studying local maps."

These details, given so easily, tended to confirm in her mind that Landon had at least been in her father's bedchamber. How else could he know the furniture, and her father's preferred drink?

"We don't have to go after Carlisle now, do we? We can take the letter straight to Sir Giles. Or to London—I had decided it was easier to get it to London, and let them handle it." A worrisome thought came to her—Landon had not known in the beginning that she was headed to Ipswich.

Even while this thought troubled her, he lifted the envelope, with a peculiar, anticipatory smile on his face. Then he tore it open and read the letter, as he had opened the other false message she gave him. He was not to be trusted after all. Despair washed over her in a wave; despair and remorse, shame at her incompetence, her failure.

"That is marked private!" she said, reaching to grab at it.

He caught her hand and held it tightly. He did no more than glance at the closely-written pages, then he went to the bed table, lit a kindling stick and held the letter to its flame. She made futile grabs at it, while he laughed and held her off. The precious letter, for which she had risked her life, and suffered so many indignities, was reduced to a wisp of ash that floated on the air.

"Traitor!" she said, tears of frustration starting in her eyes. "I was right about you all along. You're as bad as Carlisle—worse!" Her hands curled into fists; she flailed against his chest. It was like beating a wall. He even seemed amused at her puny efforts at revenge.

"Those are harsh words, my dear," he said with a gloating, satisfied smile. "Put on your shoes; we're leaving."

CHAPTER
Fourteen

*I*T HARDLY MATTERED that the sole of her shoe was flapping. It matched the rest of her ludicrous ensemble. She did not bother to ask where they were going. Her mission was lost. If she were to be killed, it was no more than she deserved. Her father had trusted her, for the first time in her life she had a chance to accomplish something worthwhile, and she had failed.

"Can we not find a bonnet to do justice to your *haut couture?*" he asked, the French phrase falling easily from his tongue. Of course it would—French conversations would be no mystery to him, nor French newspapers. His complexion too was dark, swarthy, like a Latin. While he spoke, he directed a laughing gaze on her mutinous face.

"A *French* bonnet would suit your taste best, would it not?"

"Let us give credit where credit is due. They *do* create the most elegant bonnets."

"I did not realize it was yourself you were exculpating when you spoke so highly of French spies working for

France. How did you manage to get into my father's bedroom?''

"By the door," he answered facetiously.

"If you've harmed him, Kiley . . ."

"Landon, ma'am, *s'il vous plaît.*"

"More likely Ladonnée, I suspect."

"Try this, Nessie," he suggested, picking up her bonnet and batting it against his leg to shake off the balls of dust. "You take me for a Frenchie? Should I be flattered, I wonder? They *do* have the reputation for a certain flair for style I have never been accused of before. Truth to tell, I hardly speak the bongjaw at all. I can read it, but my pronunciation is execrable."

"You *write* your reports back home, do you?"

"Now, *really!*" he said, shaking his head at her.

She tried to think of any possible revenge she could take on this hateful, deceitful man. Her eyes went around the room, while his followed them. He was still smiling. "Pity Mrs. Euston does not keep a traveling clock on her dresser," he said, rubbing his temple. "That was a nasty blow, Vanessa. Fortunate for my vanity my hair conceals the bump. A regular goose egg. Would you like to examine the damage you have done me?"

"No, sir, I would like to add to it."

"Don't be a ninny. Come along, and put on your shoes like a good girl."

She stood firm, refusing to budge. "We are still in a hurry, you know," he pointed out, dragging her by the arm to the bed, where he shoved her down quite roughly. "I am no Prince Charming, to put them on for you and have my brains bashed in while I am literally at your feet. Put them on at once, or you'll go barefoot to London."

The shoes were shoved into her hands. There was an urgency in his speech, but of more interest was the reference to London. If he did plan to take her there, it was a better spot to find help than here, in an isolated cottage in the wilds. She put on the shoes, stood up, glaring at him, lifted up the long skirt of Mrs. Euston's gown and went to the door, with Kiley right behind her. They went downstairs in silence; Kiley took a quick, fairly disinterested look at a man who was tied up on the parlor floor, said, "*Au revoir, mon ami,*" with a pleasant smile, then turned to the front door to open it for her. Just before he did so, he stepped back and regarded her toilette.

"I think, just a trifle this way," he said, tilting her bonnet over her right eye. "We want to appear in the highest style on our first outing together."

She sniffed and jerked her head away. "Careful, my pet," he warned, turning her head back by putting one finger under her chin. "You are in supreme danger of being kissed. I am beginning to find your pouts nearly as stimulating as danger."

She wrenched open the door and hurried out, while a little trail of laughter followed her. The boy, Bobbie, sat in the seat of Kiley's curricle, which hardly surprised her. She was coming to think nothing could surprise her now. If she was told Carlisle and Kiley were bosom bows, working together, she would have believed it.

"Why are you wearing Grandma's dress?" he asked her.

"Because Grandma tore hers," Kiley answered for her.

"Finished tearing it to shreds, after *you* were kind enough to begin the job," she told him.

Bobbie jumped down, throwing the reins to Kiley.

"I'll buy you a new one," he offered, his good humor unimpaired; then he turned back to the boy. "Your friend and I are playing a little game. I'm the constable and he's a crook. You'll find him tied up in the parlor. Maybe he'll give you some tea if you free him."

"Millie ran away," he said. "Tompkins doesn't make my tea. Millie makes it."

"Any idea where she ran to?" he asked.

"Yes, she ran home. Shall I go after her? I'm very hungry. She doesn't live far away."

"Sure, you go after her. We'll let Tompkins stay tied up."

"Maybe I better untie Tompkins first," he decided. He went into the house, while Kiley turned back to Vanessa.

"Poor little beggar." He handed her into a curricle. "Like it?" he asked, admiring the handsome yellow rig.

"I had to steal it from the stable yard at Colchester. I left in a bit of a hurry, and had only an old jade with me."

"You managed to kill the constable, did you?"

"Constable? I don't understand your meaning. Being hit on the head by a clock is not against the law."

"I refer to the constable Carlisle sent for to have you arrested after you beat him up."

"He must have forgotten to do it. There was no constable to contend with."

"He did not forget. I was there when he sent the inn boy after him. Are you a constitutional liar? There can be no point in denying it."

"Carlisle did not stick around to press any charges. When I came to, after a *merciless* blow to the head, Carlisle was gone. Checked out. Of equal importance, Mrs. Euston had left. As she had just arrived a short while before with a very weary team of nags, which were still at the inn's stable, I took the brilliant notion of going to the other hostelry in town, where I spotted her just leaving. I learned her direction by watching her carriage till it had turned on to the main road."

"You knew I was with her, then?"

"But of course, my dear. Would I be likely to let you and your precious letter out of my sight for long?" he asked in a mock-sympathetic way.

"I can't imagine how Carlisle and Mrs. Euston got out of the inn without my seeing them. I watched the front door from a shop across the street."

"Inns *do* have back doors."

"You took your time in following me."

"True, a regrettable lapse on my part, but I did have to make arrangements to steal this rig, you see. It wasn't done in a minute. First I had to discover who owned it, then tell the stable hands to have Mr. Brown's rig brought around, then there was a demmed pesky groom who came with it, and *he* had to be disposed of. He took the peculiar idea Mr. Brown might dislike my borrowing it."

"Did you kill him, the groom?"

"I am not so violent. A taste of the home-brewed was

sufficient to convince him of Mr. Brown's wishes in the matter.''

"I don't find this a subject for levity, Mr. Kiley."

"You use the name on purpose to vex me. Landon—Colonel Landon. As we are such close friends and conspirators, however, you may call me Stan. That is short for Stanier, not Stanley, by the by. Would you like me to call you Vanessa, or Nessie, as your aunt does?''

''My name is Miss Bradford.''

"That is so very formal, and Brad is not at all euphonious, is it? Missie, perhaps,'' he said as they trotted briskly down the sheepwalk to the main road. She waited with some curiosity to see if he did indeed turn toward London, or whether that too was a lie.

"We actually *are* going toward London, are we?'' she asked when he executed the proper turn.

"They will be interested to hear where and when Boney plans to pop in for his long-awaited visit.''

"Is that what was in the letter?'' she asked, so startled she forgot to be ironic.

"You mean you didn't know!''

"I had no idea. Papa didn't tell me anything. When is he coming?''

"Probably not in the near future now, since they know we got hold of the news.''

"How do they know?''

"Carlisle knows he failed to intercept the letter. I daresay he had some inkling what it contained. He must be the man who met the French spies to inform them of local preparations near Hastings. His eagerness was to learn if the letter actually told the correct time and date. If so, the invasion date would have to be changed. He must have followed you from home, and if he hung out there, he would know your father's habit of walking the beach at night. Forrester, the idiot, had no more wits than to broadcast it as a famous joke. Nepotism is the curse of England. If he weren't nephew to . . . But that is quite a different hobbyhorse of mine. If there was the slightest chance your father had stumbled upon this news, it had to be confirmed. If the letter dealt with some other matter, then the

invasion could go forward as planned. That is not why I
burned it, however.''

She sat silent, digesting all this, and wondering how
much of it, if any, to believe.

"Are you not at all curious to learn why I did?" he
prodded.

"Of course."

"It wasn't because of the time and place of Bonaparte's
invasion, really. Your father was indiscreet enough to have
outlined in some detail his plans for the defense of the
coast. Better plans than presently exist, and ones I would
like to employ. One likes to keep the enemy as much in
the dark as possible in these matters, you know. Oh, their
spies will know the locations where the armies are mass-
ing, but certain routes and movements and plans, at least,
we can keep from them."

"*You* would like to employ?" she asked.

"I am replacing the dashing Colonel Forrester. It is why
I was on the coast at that appropriate moment. A few
hours later than was appropriate, actually."

"Why did you burn Papa's plans? We should take them
to London."

"We are taking them, in my head. It is safer than on
paper."

"You hardly looked at them."

"I should tell you what a rapid reader I am, to impress
you, but the truth is, I had a long talk with your father. I
know what the papers said. Also, I remember the time and
place where Bonaparte was to strike."

"Where are we going then? To the Foreign Office?"

"To Whitehall, where the news should have been sent
in the first place, but as your father is retired, he feared his
news would not receive the attention it deserved. General
Harkman, an old friend and superior from India, he felt
would have a better ear in London. And time, while of
course important, was not desperately short. It is an age-
old problem, the mutual distrust between politicians and
the military. As Harkman straddled the fence, with one
boot in each camp, he hit on him as the man for the job."

"You don't think we ought to go to Harkman?"

"I don't think it is necessary. I will be listened to," he said with unbecoming arrogance of which he was not even aware. "I cannot approve of Bradford's sending two ladies to do a man's job, but on the other hand, if the ladies had not stopped off to examine the ballroom, they would not have fallen into a hobble, I fancy. You would have had a good enough head start on Carlisle that he would never have overtaken you. Or perhaps he would, who knows? He would have driven all night, if necessary. In any case, your father thought sending you was the most inconspicuous manner in which to deliver the news, since he could not make the trip himself. Little did he realize the furor caused amongst the officers when it was learned Miss Bradford was not to attend the ball. The place was buzzing with it. You must be a famous flirt, Nessie."

"It was Aunt Elleri's vinaigrette that caused it," she said, realizing the triviality of the excuse. "The chemist's shop is so close to the assembly hall, that naturally we stopped in to see the decorations. They had silk tents . . ."

"Naturally," he agreed, with a disparaging eye. "Had you never seen Carlisle lurking around town?"

"No, but he would not have been wearing a scarlet tunic and shako, so . . ." She stopped short, aware again of how unconscionably flighty her words were, and how true.

"I can change as soon as we get to London," he said, biting back a grin. "You had better ingratiate me while you have the chance. I'll be top dog at the camp, commanding officer."

"Then Papa is bound to bar the door to you at Levenhurst."

"I don't think so. I do not handle matters in Forrester's dilatory fashion. We see more or less eye-to-eye on what should be done, Colonel Bradford and myself. Once a man has actually been in battle, he views war differently than an armchair soldier like Forrester. Balls and routs will not be my top priority."

"Your scarlet tunic will not do you much good with the girls, in that case, Colonel."

"Girls? Who said anything about girls? It is only one I

am interested in. I almost hesitate to use the term 'girl.'
You look more like a dowager, in that rig.''

Glancing down at Mrs. Euston's gown, she found it
hard to disagree. Clothes were an irrelevance at that moment, however. She was safe, and the message was safe.
If the colonel was forward with his unwanted attentions,
she could endure it. She leaned back against the seat,
stretched in the sunlight, feeling luxuriously alive.

"It's hard to believe it is over, the awful nightmare of
the past few days,'' she said.

"It is over, nearly,'' he answered.

"You think we might encounter Carlisle again before
we deliver the message?''

"Probably not. He has no reason to suppose I managed
to follow him, as I kept hidden. He thinks the message
was not on you, and will be darting off elsewhere looking
for it. I wonder where he'll go next.''

"We don't have to care, as long as he doesn't bother
us.''

"*I* would sleep better nights if he were behind bars. A
man like that, who would sell out his own country for
money . . . He doesn't deserve to live. We know he is in
this general vicinity—he'll never be this easy to catch
again. Besides, I owe him a little something.''

"You have more than repaid him with that *vicious*
beating he suffered at your hands.''

"Not severe enough. I should have killed him. I would
have done, had I ever imagined . . . It's a strange thing,
you know, in times of war you kill a dozen men and think
little of it, but once you are into mufti, away from battle,
killing assumes a greater importance. It is more difficult to
do, is what I mean. When you *know* someone, even if you
dislike him very cordially, he's damned hard to shoot. You
don't get to know your victims in wartime—only their
uniforms. If he's wearing the enemy's jacket, he's fair
game.''

"War has a very coarsening influence on men,'' she
said sadly. "Aunt Elleri has often mentioned it.''

"You find me coarse?'' he asked swiftly.

"Carlisle, no angel to be sure, used the word 'animal.'

Also the words 'vicious' and 'brutal.' I cannot disagree with him.''

"It is impossible to deal in a gentlemanly way with the likes of Carlisle. I would like to know what you would have had me do differently.''

"I don't know. Nothing, I guess, but it is unfortunate men must behave like animals.''

"Soldiers behave like animals so that civilians need not,'' he answered swiftly, then fell silent, an offended expression settling on his countenance. When he spoke later, it was about business.

"Have you any idea where I might look for Carlisle, after I have been to Whitehall? Did he say anything?''

"No, nothing to the point.''

"How about the woman—Euston?''

"No.'' She looked around at the countryside. "Do you not mean to have *any* balls at all when you are commandant?'' she asked after a lengthy interval.

She saw his jaw firm to a perfect square. When he turned to give her one quick glance, his eyes were darkly angry. "Try, if you can, to forget *balls,* for a few moments, Miss Bradford. I cannot believe you shared a carriage all the way from Colchester with Mrs. Euston without her having said anything that might help us.''

"She spent half the trip nagging at Bobbie to be still. Oh, she did ask rather particularly about my trunk, now that I think of it. I told her it was left on the stage, and then she wanted to know what coaching stop it was to be left at, and what time. When they didn't find the letter on me, they might have taken the idea it was in my trunk, I suppose.''

"He had already searched it once. The lining was ripped out when I got to his room that night, with your things spilled all over the place. That was why I had to rough him up a little, to discover if he had it. When he showed me the plain white paper, I realized what you had done.''

"You never told me why you opened my letter, the one I gave you at Maldon.''

"For the same reason I opened the real one. To read it,

burn it and take the news on in person, in a way Carlisle
could not get at it.''

"Oh. But I did not mean my valise. I mean my trunk
was supposed to be on the stage.''

"Your father told me you only threw a few linens into a
case.''

"We could not go away for a week without a trunk.
You never know if the Harkmans might be planning a
party, or even a ball.''

He looked at her, bewildered, but said nothing of her
vanity. "What time, and what place, did you tell Euston
your trunk would be in London?''

"Stephen's Hotel, at four o'clock. It was what the
schedule said.''

"Then she'll believe it. I doubt we'll be there in time to
meet them. *My* first stop *must* be Whitehall. That is our
top priority.''

"Are you suggesting *I* should go to the stage and see if
they are there?'' she asked, resentful at further demands on
her.

"Are you offering?'' he asked with a sarcastic lift of his
brow.

"No, I am not, and I don't think a gentleman would
even hint I should, after what I have been through.''

"You may be very sure I was not even hinting. You are
the last person in the country I would entrust with a
mission of any importance. You would doubtlessly stop to
have a new gown measured up en route.''

"What am *I* to do while you go, then?''

"You will be placed somewhere safe. You can remain
at Whitehall if you have no friends to stay with.''

"I have an aunt. I'll go to her. I cannot be seen at
Whitehall like this.''

"Don't entertain her with this tale till you hear from
me.''

"Remembering this ordeal is not my idea of entertainment, Colonel. Neither is staying with my Aunt Halford.''

He turned a scathing eye toward her. "It is a matter of
deep concern to me, of course, that you should be poorly
entertained for a few hours. I really *do* apologize. Blame it

on my military coarseness, but I feel the exigency of saving the nation from an invasion by Napoleon Bonaparte must take precedence for the next few hours. Just be patient, Miss Bradford. You will be home soon enough, with whole platoons of officers to amuse you.''

"My life is not made up of flirting with officers,'' she answered swiftly. "I lead a very dull, quiet life, with an invalid father who is bad-humored, along with all the rest.''

"Men who are in constant pain from wounds are apt to be ill-humored. I should think a dutiful daughter would make it her first business to see he is spared as much aggravation as possible.''

"I do not aggravate him.''

"I find that difficult to believe. If you do not purposely aggravate him, there is no point pretending you stir a finger to help him in his concerns. A colonel's daughter should have a stronger sense of duty. Our country is at war, in jeopardy this minute from a French invasion. You were asked to perform one small task to help, and even that you could not undertake to execute with either good-will or the least degree of competence. You have done nothing but whine at the disagreeableness of your errand and make one wrong, foolish, dangerous decision after another. Don't speak to me of entertainment, Miss Bradford. Your life has been one long entertainment. It was poor training for the job entrusted to you. One can only assume your father was blinded to your *utter* selfishness by his love for you. If you were *my* daughter, I would be ashamed of you.''

"He doesn't love me! He never has.''

"You are mistaken. He was extremely concerned for your safety. Only his sense of duty impelled him to send you. He thought you could be trusted. What else but love could be so blind?'' he asked with a blighting stare, then he returned his attention to his driving.

Vanessa squared her shoulders, ready to defend herself, but there was some rejection in the square set of his shoulders, the implacable tightening of his jaw. Why should she care for the opinion of an ill-mannered brute? Her life was not at all as he imagined it to be. She was a good and dutiful daughter. Was it *her* fault she was not trained to be a spy? She was well out of this wretched predicament. She would go to Aunt Halford and forget it, let him handle it. He was paid to.

CHAPTER
Fifteen

VANESSA WAS TIRED, and angry and uncomfortable, being bolted along too quickly in an open carriage that showed every passerby her ridiculous gown. Most of all, she was furious with Landon for daring to read her a lecture, after all she had done to help the country. That was gratitude for you! For a mile, her companion said not one single word. The silence was so oppressive it could be cut with a knife. She took short, occasional looks at his profile. She read the worried, concentrating look he wore, and knew that for him, the fight was not over yet. His thoroughness would not be satisfied till he had not only delivered the message, but apprehended Carlisle as well. And even then, there was still the war to be fought! She thought he must be a good soldier. He was effectual, clever, hard. Her father too was like that, though he was capable of tenderness upon rare occasions. He had promised her a ball, when he saw her gown hanging ready in her room. Landon too had been sympathetic for about two seconds, at Euston's cottage. Sympathy from a man like Papa or Landon meant more than from a Forrester, who was always ready to grieve for a touch of migraine or a muddied gown or a missed visit. You knew you had *earned* their commiseration, and knew they meant it too.

During one of her quick peeps, Landon turned suddenly and looked at her. She saw the haggard look around his eyes and mouth, came to realize he had not slept the night before, any more than she had herself. He too had suffered, even at her own hands. She accused him of viciousness, but she had attacked him without a qualm, hit him as hard as she could and not looked back to see if she had killed him. In desperate times, you do desperate things.

"Where does this aunt of yours live in London?" he asked, his tone chilly. She had scolded all the merriment, the elation of his little victory out of him.

"In Belgrave Square. Just leave me at Whitehall and do what you must do. They'll take me to her. I'll be safe. You don't have to worry about me any more."

"Are you asking me not to call on you? Would you prefer not to see me again?" he asked bluntly.

"No! That was not my meaning." Landon was a hard man to *like*, but she had reluctantly come to respect him, and wished he might have a better opinion of her character.

"Are you sure? I could became a great pest, with very little persuasion." A tentative smile took the rough edge from his face. How could he smile so soon after his tirade?

"I—I only meant . . . The thing is, I said more than I should have, about your behavior. You had to be brutal. I understand that. I shouldn't have criticized. In fact, I don't believe I ever apologized for hitting you."

"I understand. It is a belated attack of conscience that spurs you on to sympathy. I shall call to let you know what happens, but I shan't become a pest. Promise."

He was wearing his stiff, offended face again. Her shoulders sagged from the chore of being polite, trying not to hurt his feelings, while still not encouraging his advances. His reading of her character bothered her too, as there was more than a little truth in it. She took small heed for her father's comfort or well-being. She made no effort to control her yawns when he read those awfully long extracts about the war in India. His complaints about his chest had become boring, from repetition, but a constant pain must be hard to bear. She could help him, lighten his burden by cheerful company at least, instead of finding an excuse to leave the room shortly after he entered. Yes, she was not a very considerate daughter, but she would do better, try to become closer to him, while she still had the chance. He was no longer young.

They continued in nearly total silence to London. She felt a fool to enter gracious Whitehall decked out so grotesquely, like a lady in a farce, with her sole flapping at every step, but she did not mention it for fear of another outburst from Landon. What did it matter anyway? No one was paying any attention to her.

The first clerk they met recognized Landon. "Colonel, you back so soon!" he exclaimed. "I hope it doesn't mean trouble on the coast?"

"Shh, the walls have ears. I have to see the secretary of war, at once," he answered.

"He is at a meeting at 10 Downing. Shall I fetch him?"

"If you would be so kind. It's urgent."

With no more than a word from the colonel, the clerk hastened off to interrupt a meeting of the Cabinet. She was amazed to see her companion was taken so seriously, was so important a person in London. A request was easy to make, however. Whether the secretary of state for war would come trotting was another matter.

It was not only the secretary of state for war who came, but the Foreign Secretary and the prime minister himself, along with a clutch of high-ranking military officers. "Landon, what is it?" one of the military men asked.

"General Almont," Landon said, springing to attention and saluting. "We had best speak in private."

Vanessa sat forgotten on her chair. No one noticed her grotesque gown, her torn shoe. She might have been a flyspeck on the wall, for all the attention paid her. As the group of men turned in a great bustle to depart, Landon remembered her. "Will someone look after Miss Bradford?" he asked the clerk.

"Simmons, attend to the lady," the officer ordered with a questioning glance at the bizarre apparition that stared at him from the chair.

"Keep a close watch on her. She might possibly still be in some danger," Landon added. "Perhaps . . ." He turned to one of the men in the group, a young, pale gentleman who looked not important. She thought he was to be despatched as her protector. Some words were whispered between them, then they both stepped toward her.

"The prime minister would like to thank you, Miss Bradford," Landon said.

She gulped and arose, to receive the thanks of the first minister of the country. She could not think of a word to say. "You're welcome," she said with a curtsey, feeling her speech entirely inadequate to the honor of the occasion. They were gone before she quite realized what august company she had been in.

She looked at their retreating forms, feeling excluded from important and very interesting goings-on. She did not quite forget it was her own wish that she be taken to her aunt, yet it seemed hard that she must miss out on the denouement of the adventure. Landon, in his usual arrogant, overbearing way was assuming control of the whole, bending prime minister and all of officialdom to his whim. It was *her* father who had sent the letter. She felt very much abused.

"The colonel didn't waste a minute, did he?" the clerk commented with an approving smile. "It was a wise decision to send him down to the coast, though I think it severe he was not given some time off after his return from India."

"Is that where he has been? He never said so. I wondered why he was so dark."

"Indeed yes. Have you not been reading of his exploits amongst the Marathas?"

"No, I haven't followed it," she answered, knowing she displayed her ignorance. India was so far away, and wars with Indians, despite her father's following the matter with the greatest concern, had never interested her.

"Young ladies have more entertaining things to do with their time," the clerk answered, not disapprovingly, but with calm acceptance of ladies' folly. "Now, what can I do for you, Miss Bradford? Would you like me to take you somewhere?"

"I have to go to Belgrave Square."

"I shall arrange for a couple of Guards to accompany you. The colonel mentioned you might be in some danger."

She was not at all eager for a pair of elegant Guards to see her in Mrs. Euston's gown. In fact, she did not want to go to Aunt Halford at all, to sit in a saloon sipping tea and talking with an elderly and very boring gossip, while Landon went chasing Carlisle, doing *her* duty for her.

Her country was in peril, and what was her contribution? To wound and obstruct in every way the man who was trying to save it, the man who had the prime minister running at a word. She could at least go to the stage stop and see if Carlisle and Mrs. Euston were there. With a pair of Guards to protect her and to arrest them, there would be no real danger in it, and it would give Landon a better opinion of her mettle. She realized then how much she wanted his good opinion.

Even while these thoughts ran through her mind, two very capable-looking gentlemen, not in uniform but in ordinary blue jackets, bustled past. "He said four o'clock. We'll never make it. They'll have asked for the trunk and gone."

"The stage is always late," the other answered. "Bond Street stop, wasn't it?"

"That's what he said."

They were gone, rushing out the door. Landon had remembered to handle the matter, with no help from her. A glance at her watch showed her it wanted only two minutes of four. They would not make it unless the stage was very late indeed.

"I'm going with them," she said, taking the decision on the spur of the moment.

"Wait! Colonel Landon said . . ."

"I'll be safe with two men to guard me," she called over her shoulder.

She flapped along after them, stumbling at every second step with her torn shoe. She caught them up, panting wildly, just as they were climbing into a carriage.

"This must be Miss Bradford," one of them said, smiling at her outfit.

"Yes, I shall go to the stage stop with you. I can identify them."

"Spring 'em," he called to the driver as she hopped in. "That's a good idea. We have their description from Landon, but a positive identification would help, particularly if they are in disguise."

"Yes, and I know what the groom and footman look like too—the men on Mrs. Euston's carriage."

"Do you know, Rob," the elder of the gentlemen said to the other, "I *do* believe the golden-haired boy has slipped up on one item. Landon didn't mention a groom and footman, did he?"

"He has *much more* important things on his mind!" she retorted hotly. Why was she not pleased to hear of his making a slip? Why did she feel this urgent compulsion to defend him?

The driver took his order to spring 'em seriously. The dash through the city traffic was hair-raising. It was also futile. They did not arrive at the stop till well after four. There was no sign of either Carlisle, Mrs. Euston, groom or footman.

"I'll ask if anyone has been enquiring for your trunk," the elder man said, then strode quickly to the wicket.

"There was an elderly dame in black asking for it," he reported a minute later.

"Mrs. Euston," she said. "I wonder where she would have gone from here."

"London is a big city. It would be like looking for a needle in a haystack. We'd best report back to Landon."

"He had some men sent back to that cottage where Miss Bradford was taken, in case they return there. That will be their destination, don't you think?" he asked her.

"Very likely. They left a boy there." She felt in her bones it must be so. Mrs. Euston's scolding of Bobbie indicated concern as well as impatience.

"Where shall we drop you off, ma'am?" he asked next.

"Belgrave Square," she answered, despondent.

CHAPTER
Sixteen

*H*ER ARRIVAL AT the home of the Halfords in Belgrave Square caused a major shock. "Vanessa—my dear, what in the *world* . . . !" Mrs. Halford exclaimed, looking at her bedraggled appearance. Aunt Halford had a concern for fashion not far behind Elleri Simons. Her gown and coiffure were of the latest kick, but her sagging face and overstuffed body did nothing to enhance them.

"It is a long story, Auntie. Could I have a bath and borrow some clean clothes before I tell you the whole? To satisfy your curiosity, I shall just tell you I have had a very disagreeable few days."

"But what happened?"

"I was kidnapped," she answered. "I managed to escape—that is, I was rescued by a Colonel Landon, whom my father sent after me."

"Colonel Landon! Nessie, what marvelous luck! He will fall in love with you for a certainty. So very handsome and clever. All of London is puffing him up, since he is come home from India covered with medals and ribbons. What is he like?"

"He is rather like Papa," she replied, with a bemused smile. "He is not particularly handsome. In fact, I found him plain, at first," she added, with a smile that suggested her like of plainness.

"Yes, my dear, but what is he *like*?"

"You may judge for yourself when he comes to call. I expect he may be here this evening."

"Coming *here*? Delightful! I'll be the envy of them all. Sit down this instant and tell me *all* about it," her aunt commanded, her brightly curious eyes shining in her sagging face. "Wine—we shall have a glass of wine while you tell me."

Without much reluctance, Vanessa sat down and accepted a glass of wine. "I cannot tell you everything. It is to do with Bonaparte, you see. Top secret."

"I knew you were in great jeopardy on the coast. You ought to have come to me *months* ago, when first the villain began building those nasty flatboats."

"I could not leave Papa alone, and you know what chance there would be of dragging him away when he had such exciting things to do at home."

"That is true. Henry is a fire horse. When he sees an army preparing, he reaches for his musket. I think he *likes* fighting and shooting and killing people."

"Someone has to do it," Vanessa answered sharply. "*I* think he is a hero."

"Never mind that, but only tell me all about your kidnapping."

"Aunt Elleri and myself had to . . . Oh, dear, Aunt Elleri! I have scarcely given her a thought since morning. I hope she is all right."

"Where is she? Was she not kidnapped with you? No, of course she was not, or she would be here. Landon would never rescue you and leave her behind."

"No, he thinks of everything."

"I should hope so indeed. A fine hero that would be, to leave her behind. Where is she?"

"At Colchester."

"The widgeon, going off on a visit just when you need her. I never thought her a proper chaperone for you,

Nessie. She thinks of nothing but gowns and shoes, and a *very* unattractive outfit she has chosen too, if you will forgive my saying so, dear. You must not be seen in public in such an ancient gown. It don't fit at all well. You will be comdemned as a quiz.''

"William Pitt did not take exception to it!''

"I never heard *he* had set up as an arbiter of style,'' was her comment upon hearing her niece had spoken to the prime minister. "What is she doing at Colchester?'' was the next question.

"I don't know,'' Vanessa replied, her mind beginning to explore this question. Soon she had an awful vision of what her aunt would be doing in the very near future. Carlisle would discover there was no trunk on the stage—had already discovered it. He would scan the possible places the letter could be, and he would conclude it was still in Colchester. He would go back, and her poor aunt sat like a fly in a web, with no notion the man was a scoundrel.

"I have got to leave,'' she said, arising up from her chair.

"Yes, my dear, I shall have the servants draw a hot bath, but about your adventure . . .''

"I need the loan of your carriage, Auntie, and a couple of stout footmen.''

"Nessie! *Female* servants will help you with your bath.''

"I am not taking a bath now. I have to go out.''

"You cannot be seen on the streets in that anachronism of a gown. There is no point asking it. I forbid it. Loose black robes are not at all the thing this or any other year.''

"I should send a note to Colonel Landon, telling him where I am, in case he does not think of it. But of course he will,'' she added with a perfectly confident smile.

"He *knows* you are here, child. You said he would call this evening.''

"Where I am going, is what I mean.''

"You are not going anywhere but upstairs to have a bath and get out of that ugly robe. Mine will not fit much better, but at least they ain't black.''

"Auntie, it is a matter of life and death.''

"I know, Nessie, but there is no death in the family, so there is no need to wear black. Goodness, as if I did not know at my age that black is worn for mourning."

"Please call your carriage. I must go at once."

"I will not do any such foolish thing."

"Then I must, and pray do not forbid it, or I shall steal it, as Landon did."

"What, Landon steal my carriage? You are mad. He did nothing of the sort. I would have noticed if one was missing. I only have the two."

Without further ado, Vanessa bolted from the room to ask the butler to have the carriage brought around immediately, with two of the strongest footmen in the house ready to accompany her. Her aunt was at her heels, forbidding loudly.

"My dear aunt, if you want Miss Simons' death on your head, then withhold your carriage. I promise you I will run into the street and take the first one I find standing idle."

"Vanessa, you will land in Bridewell."

"Then you had better let me have your rig."

"She has run mad. Totally demented. Call the carriage. I wash my hands of her."

"Will you come with me?" Vanessa asked as she waited for the carriage's appearance at the door.

"Certainly not. I am attending a ball this evening."

"That sounds familiar," Miss Bradford said.

"Really? What ball are you attending?"

"None."

"You are perfectly welcome to come if you wish. Maybe Colonel Landon will stand up with you. He is bound to be there if he is in town. Everyone was bemoaning his departure."

"He won't be there."

Till the carriage appeared, Vanessa listened to the most foolish and irrelevant series of remarks she had heard since leaving her aunt at Colchester. Several scandalous pieces of gossip were told her, but she was not listening. She was thinking that at last she was doing something Colonel Landon would approve of. He would realize she was not just a selfish, silly girl, but a woman of character.

"Do you have a gun?" was the only thing she said to her aunt.

"Of course I have a gun. I would not be without a gun in the house. I do not allow any ammunition, however. It would be much too dangerous. Someone could get hurt."

"Never mind. I'll stop and find a constable before I go to the inn."

"Nessie, where are you going that you require a gun? You must *not* rob an inn, my dear. If you are short of funds, I will be happy to help you out till quarter day. Your reputation will be in tatters if you get caught."

"I don't intend to get caught this time."

"*This time!* Are you brass-faced enough to stand and tell me to my face you make a *habit* of it! Dear God, and using my carriage. I will be taken for an accomplice. I shall end up on the gibbet. I know it." Aunt Halford sank on to a chair and fanned herself strenuously with a limp handkerchief. She was not at all sorry to see the back of her niece. The girl had run mad, and it was a great pity she should be using her own carriage to execute her wild scheme. Colonel Landon would be disgusted with her. An excellent *parti* lost to the family. Her next thought was how she could conceal having any part in the affair herself. If they said in the papers her carriage had been used, she would sue. No, she wouldn't, though. She would report it missing, at once! Stolen from the stables, but not by her niece, of course.

With the two sturdy footmen mounted behind and a hefty groom handling the ribbons, the carriage was off. They had been given the direction and told to drive at top speed. Getting out of London was the slowest and most annoying part of the trip. Vanessa went over her plan, testing to see if she was correct to return to Colchester. Carlisle had searched herself and her belongings and not found the letter. He would go back to the cottage first to look for it—to try to force the information from her. Seeing she had escaped, he *must* assume the letter was still back at the inn at Colchester. Where else could it possibly be? He might think she had put it in the post, but he would at least go back and try his luck at the inn. He would suspect Elleri Simons had taken over its delivery. He would follow her if she had left, and if she were still there . . . Well, she knew now how Carlisle operated.

She should have told Elleri where she was going, before she left. What must her poor aunt have been thinking, all that long day? At least she had been in no danger. Not till Carlisle got back would the danger occur. She looked at her watch, wondering, worrying that he would be there before her.

Once out of city traffic, the pace increased till she was being bounced helplessly around in the carriage, like a rag doll in a child's wagon. Ordinarily, it might have made her ill, but on this occasion she felt such a sense of exhilaration and danger she did not mind in the least. Her only regret was that she was alone. It would have been more enjoyable with Colonel Landon by her side. She thought he would not be far behind her. Frequent looks out the carriage window failed to find him. There were many yellow curricles, but the one stolen from Mr. Brown was not amongst them.

As they approached the side road leading to Mrs. Euston's cottage, she pulled the check string to slow the carriage, but there was no sign of either Carlisle or the men Landon had sent. Her best chance of beating Carlisle to Colchester was to plunge on, and really she was not at all eager to see again the scene of her misery. When the team slowed down from fatigue, they stopped to change horses. They were at the midpoint of their trip. No one there had any information about Carlisle having passed, but this was hardly remarkable. There were many choices of a stop. She took advantage of the delay to speak to the footmen, who were to help her.

"One of you is to stop off at the constable's office in Colchester and bring an armed officer to the inn. The other will come with me inside. We shall speak to the clerk there and see where my aunt is, and whether Carlisle or Mrs. Euston has been asking for her. He is extremely dangerous. Till the armed constable arrives, we shall do nothing but discover his location. I shall listen at my aunt's door, and if the situation is desperate, if they are threatening or hurting her, I'll pound on the door and create a disturbance. Very likely they will have a gun to loan me at the inn," she said hopefully.

The footmen settled between them which was to run for the constable, and they both agreed an inn would not be without a weapon. She felt very brave and efficient as she made all the arrangements for her aunt's rescue and the villains' capture. She was undecided in her mind whether it would be more glorious to present Landon with a *fait accompli*, hand the prisoners to him in manacles, or to let him watch with wonder as she managed the affair with the *sangfroid* of a seasoned campaigner. Having a fair notion which of them would do the managing if he were present, she decided her preference was to accomplish the entire deed before his arrival.

She got back into the carriage, the footmen mounted behind, and they continued on their way, their pace quickened again with the fresh team. It was already evening when they reached the town. Having no idea where the constable's office was to be found, they drove down the main street once, without discovering it. They had to stop to enquire of a pedestrian, who pointed up a side street. One would think the constable would be located on the main street, easy to find. The chosen footman hopped down from his perch at the carriage's rear to deliver an armed constable to them, at top speed. The carriage returned to the inn.

The lobby was busy, with dinner guests descending from their rooms, and others coming in off the street. The clerk was not at his post at the desk. After several minutes' searching, he was found, and condescended to examine his records. Yes, a Miss Simons was still registered in the White Rose Suite.

"Have you seen her about recently?" Vanessa asked.

Very scanty civility was offered a young lady who stood before the clerk in what he supposed to be her grandmother's gown. Had she not been accompanied by a liveried footman, she felt sure she would have been politely requested to leave the premises.

"My dear young lady," the clerk said, "I do not recog-

nize by sight every client who stops with us for a day or
two. She is registered—that is all I can tell you. Go to her
suite, and see if she is in."

"*Naturally* I mean to do so," she retaliated, her eyes
flashing, "and I shall report your insolence to the proprietor as well."

"I *am* the proprietor."

She sniffed. "Then will you be good enough to tell me
if Mr. Carlisle is also registered," she said, in her loftiest
manner.

"Mr. Carlisle has been registered for two days, miss."

"He left this morning."

"You are mistaken. I saw him not a quarter of an hour
ago. I could well do without such customers as Carlisle
and Kiley, making disturbance in my rooms, calling constables, annoying my clients."

"Is Kiley here too?" she asked, her heart lurching in
hope despite her daydream of settling the business without
him.

"He slipped out last night, before the boy arrived with
the constable."

"If he comes back, tell him to go directly to Miss
Simons' suite."

"If he comes back, I shall personally usher him out the
door."

"You must not!"

His supercilious smile deteriorated to a sneer. "Is there
anything else, miss?"

She tossed her head and left, without replying. Then she
went at a dragging gait to the stairway. "You had better
go back and ask him for a gun," she said to the footman.
She knew he would not hand it over to her if he had one.

"Yes, ma'am," the footman said. The alacrity with
which he departed told her he was no more eager for the
coming confrontation than she was herself. Really it made
much better sense to wait for the constable's arrival. She
looked up the stairs, looked around the lobby for a sign of
Carlisle, half hoping and half dreading she would see him.
At least she knew he was here, and he did *not* know she
was. That gave her a slight advantage. She looked back to

the desk, to see the footman pleading with the clerk, who shook his head in a determined negative. Whoever thought it would be so difficult to be a heroine? The whole world was in league to prevent her. And why did not the constable come? He was only a few blocks away.

Meanwhile, her aunt sat alone and unaware of the danger Carlisle presented. Vanessa would tiptoe up to her door and put her ear to it. There could not be much danger in that. If all was silent, she would enter, and tell Elleri she must bar her door at once, or possibly it would be best for them to go down to the busy lobby. She went reluctantly up the stairs, looked down the empty hallway to a series of closed doors. One opened, causing her flesh to crawl with fear. It was only a lady and gentleman who came out, laughing and talking together.

"They must be drunk," the lady said.

"Shocking behavior. The world's going to the dogs," the man answered.

Vanessa discerned no importance in these speeches. While the couple were still in view, offering some security by their mere presence, she scampered quickly to her aunt's door. There was silence within. She reached for the knob, then decided it would be better to peek in the keyhole first, as a precaution. The two customers had passed on down the stairs from view. She bent down, to see the key was in the hole, blocking her view. The reassuring silence assumed a menacing aura. Suppose Carlisle had already been and gone—done his work, left Elleri wounded, or dead. Her brow was damp with fear, and within her body was a quaking that set every limb trembling. Did soldiers feel like this before a battle? she wondered.

CHAPTER
Seventeen

*H*ER SHAKING FINGERS reached for the knob; before they touched it, a voice raised in anger issued through the door. She jumped back as though she had been burned. The voice was followed by a loud rattle, as someone—surely not Elleri!—hit the door. It shook in its frame, before her eyes. Fear, caution, common sense—all were overcome in the fraction of a second. She hardly trembled as she flung the door wide and took a step inside. Her first view was of her aunt, safe for the moment but backed cowering into a corner, with a look of helpless terror in her eyes.

"What have you done to her?" she demanded, turning to the left, where a shadow of a man had already been seen from the corner of her eye.

"Colonel Landon!" she exclaimed joyfully, till she noticed his expression was very little different from her aunt's.

"Get out!" he shouted. He held a pistol, which was aimed in her direction. Her world was turned upside down again. Would she *never* sort out this muddle?

"I will not!"

There was a blurring movement just at the edge of her vision. A man slid silently out from behind the door, grabbed her arm and pulled her in front of him. It was not necessary to look to know his identity. Of course it was Carlisle. His voice confirmed it.

"Throw it down, Landon," he said.

Landon hesitated an instant, a wary, calculating light in his eyes.

"Toss it on to the bed, or your lady friend is dead."

Landon threw his pistol to the bed. Elleri Simons looked from one of them to the other, while Vanessa too surveyed the scene around her, looking for Mrs. Euston. If Carlisle was alone, surely the three of them could overpower him. She noticed the window was open, the curtains blowing in the breeze. One of the men had entered by that means, thus avoiding any curious onlookers in the hallway or lobby.

He would also have failed to see a constable, surely arriving by now. Why wasn't Mrs. Euston here? She would be awaiting below, with the carriage set to bolt. Carlisle was going to keep herself propped in front of him till he got out, then he would either push her aside or kill her. In either case, she had been a hindrance to Landon again, when she had wanted so much to help. He would have handled Carlisle very competently by himself. That body hitting the door when she arrived showed clearly which way the fight had been going. Now he was held helpless at gunpoint, unable to make a move, for fear of getting herself killed. His eyes focused on the small black hole of Carlisle's gun, reminding her of a snake readying itself to strike its victim.

The gun shifted, taking careful aim at Landon. She saw Landon's eyes shift with it, and had an intuition what was about to happen. There was a debt to be settled between the two men; Landon had not only kept the letter from him, he had given him a sound thrashing into the bargain. He was right to have said he should have killed him while he had the chance. Now the chance was in the other hand,

and it was not an opportunity that would be passed up. What could be done about it? Nothing.

She gazed at Landon, helpless, horrified, paralyzed with grief and anxiety. She noticed he still followed the gun, his eyes steady, with some fear perhaps, but more of anger. He lifted his gaze to direct one short, sharp, commanding glance at her. What did he mean her to do? Carlisle held her, helpless, the gun not six inches from her—but not pointed *at* her. She had about three seconds between making a move and being shot. She looked back, understanding his meaning. She gave one sharp nod of her head to show him she understood, then jerked suddenly sideways, violently, pulling Carlisle and the gun with her. A loud retort rang out, echoing hideously in the chamber, and at the same instant, Landon leapt forward to tackle Carlisle. She closed her eyes, shivering uncontrollably. When she opened them, Landon lay at her feet, the blood trickling from his temple onto the carpet. Elleri groaned and slumped away in a faint.

So much happened within the next few seconds that her head was spinning, looking first to the doorway, where sounds were coming in, running, shouting sounds. A constable and the footman who had gone after him were there, both carrying guns. The uppity clerk and the other footman were also there, also with guns. Soon other heads popped up behind them, but she was not aware of this. Elleri opened her eyes, looked around and shrieked. Carlisle was escaping—halfway out the window already. With a quickness born of desperation, Vanessa ran to the window and slammed it down on his leg, pinning him to the spot while the constable ran to grab hold of his boot.

"Somebody run around to the balcony and get him. He's wiggling out of his boot," the constable ordered.

A footman ran out, the gun waving dangerously in the air.

"If there is a carriage waiting below, stop it! It is his accomplice," Vanessa called after him. The other footman ran out, happy to be involved in such excitement, now that the great part of the danger was past.

She went to bend over Landon's prostrate form, to feel

his pulse and heart for signs of life. Elleri ran to her side to stare in disapproval at the inert form. "If he's dead . . ." Vanessa said, then stopped. Her mind refused to continue, would not accept the unacceptable.

"I hope he is!" Elleri said, with the greatest relish.

"Someone—call a doctor," Vanessa said, sparing a moment to look up at the throng around the door. It was swelling to a crowd. A man went off to do as she asked, a patron of the inn, she thought.

More chaos followed. Men she had never seen before pushed their way through the crowd, making important sounds of "Stand aside!" They were stalwart, compelling gentlemen, wearing the face of officialdom. They took charge of the shambles, put out the mere curiosity seekers. They were efficient, unemotional, reassuring types. They lifted Landon onto her aunt's bed, told her unequivocally he was not dying. They outlined briefly that they had come with him from London, had been waiting at various spots outside to apprehend Carlisle if he tried to escape.

"His female accomplice is already in custody," they told her.

"Everything was under control till your unexpected entry," one added with a rebukeful glance.

"Why didn't you come in with him? Why did you let him come alone?" she retorted.

"Lady, you don't *give* Colonel Landon orders; you *take* them, if you know what's good for you."

"It didn't seem necessary," the other explained. "We saw from the window that Carlisle was in the room alone, rummaging through drawers and furnishings. He'd left the window open, to escape quickly if he heard Miss Simons at the door. We saw the carriage waiting below, took command of it and arrested the female. Colonel Landon took the decision to go in by the door and arrest him, but the instant he sneaked in, the lady came back to her room."

"I was only gone down to demand some service," Miss Simons said. "I rang and rang the bell for a quarter of an hour, and no one came to tend me, so I went downstairs to give them a piece of my mind. When I returned, the place was a shambles. Landon had rummaged through my most personal items," she added, stiff with disapproval. "The whole affair is his fault, and *I* for one am happy to see him rewarded as he deserves. He was *beating* poor Mr. Carlisle again, Nessa."

"No, it was *our* fault," Vanessa told her. "If we had done as Father asked, none of this would have happened. It was stopping at the assembly hall that did the damage."

"Well, then it is Henry's fault for sending us in the first place. Was I to make a trip without a vinaigrette? I am sure *I* have done nothing but what I thought for the best."

"No one is blaming you," Vanessa said.

"*You* just did! You may be sure Henry will try to dump the whole in my dish as well. My vinaigrette—I must have it before I swoon away from nervous exhaustion."

"It would be best to take the lady to another room," one of the officials suggested, with an impatient look at the jabbering lady.

"An excellent idea! I do not mean to share a bed with a man who is bleeding all over the pillows," Miss Simons replied, between sniffs from her vinaigrette. "We shall go to your room, Nessa."

Vanessa lingered by the bedside, disliking to leave. "Take her along. It is for the best," he advised.

"I am not leaving Colonel Landon," she announced, her firm manner making it clear she was not going to be balked.

Landon's eyes fluttered open. "Don't kill him," he said. She thought he was delirious. "Don't let them kill Carlisle."

"I hope they do!"

"I want to question him," he said, his voice weak, then he closed his eyes again, giving a good impression of a dead man. Even half dead, he was planning. She shook her head with a rueful smile.

"Did you hear him?" she asked the closest official.

"Yes, I'd best run along and see they do as he says. There'll be the almighty devil to pay if he's disobeyed."

"How did you all get here so early?" she asked the one

remaining. "I hurried straight from London as fast as I could. I made sure I would be the first to arrive."

"We rode our mounts, ma'am. The colonel thought it would be faster, as it was, of course, though I must say it was a hard gallop."

"I'm surprised they let him into the inn. He—caused a little commotion last time he was here."

"He often does." The man laughed. "I fancy that is why he went straight from the stable to the balcony. I wondered at the time, but I figured he'd done his reconnaissance in advance, and he don't like to be pestered with questions when he is busy. 'We'll check out the stable to see if Carlisle's or the woman's rig is here, and if it is, I'll go in by the window,' he told us. He changed his mind and used the door, in the end. It's awkward going in by the window unless the room's empty, you see. It gives the other a chance to have at you while you're off balance."

"He cannot have spent long at Whitehall."

"Just long enough to tell his story and make sure they knew what to do on the coast—in case he didn't come back, you know."

"He would think of that. He thinks of everything."

"He did not think *you* would be coming here," the man said with a quizzing smile. "He sent a brace of Guards over to Belgrave Square to look after you when he learned you'd scampered down to the stage stop without telling him. He feared Carlisle might have spotted you there and followed you to your aunt's home. Well, I guess you had given the Euston woman your address in any case. You must have left already by the time they got there."

"Yes. I dread to think what my aunt will think when the Guards land in. She will make sure they plan to take me to the Tower for beheading. I would have done better to stay put."

"One is generally better off to do exactly as the colonel says," he agreed. "I took the notion, from little things he said, that you were not at all anxious to come up against Carlisle again. Funny he would have misunderstood your intention. He don't usually, but then, he more usually deals with men. They don't change their minds," he added simply.

"One hesitates to utter a word of criticism, but I believe he has something to learn in the handling of ladies."

"He's learning fast. Hounding the poor mortal to death in London. It's because of his being a hero and all."

"Why doesn't that doctor come?" she scolded, finding she did not care at all for the official gentleman.

"He'll live, ma'am. It will take more than a scratch to stop him."

The doctor arrived very soon after, at which time Vanessa was told politely to wait in the next room.

CHAPTER
Eighteen

*W*HEN SHE WENT to the other room, she found her aunt had been preparing a list of sins against her over the past day. She lay stretched out on the bed, with the vinaigrette at the ready in her hand, a handkerchief in the other and a very wounded expression on her face. She launched into a sea of complaints.

"I should like to know, miss, why you went sneaking off on me in the middle of the night, without so much as a note left to inform me of your whereabouts. Have you *any idea* what my day has been like? Finding you gone, I went to call on Carlisle, to find he also had fled. Kiley the same. I even ventured to tap on *his* door. I made sure you had eloped to Scotland with Harvey, for you remember we had spoken of it. I particularly cautioned against it. I sent our carriage off to the north, looking for you, which left *me* stranded here alone, without even a carriage, and with a constable asking all manner of impertinent questions I could not answer. Why had Carlisle left, after calling him in the middle of the night? Where was Kiley? What was *our* relationship with the pair of them? I was never so humiliated in my life. You must *not* breathe a word of it to Henry."

There was a good deal more of the same, a whole litany of grievances. She could not like to walk on the streets of a strange town unaccompanied, the servants at the inn were insolent, she had the choice of eating alone in her room or rubbing elbows with cits and commoners below-stairs. "And furthermore," she finished in a final burst of anger, "you broke my good traveling clock before you left."

"Are you not curious to hear why I left so suddenly?" Vanessa asked, when she could get a word in edgewise.

"Have I not been *asking* you for the past half hour?"

"No, Auntie, you have been telling me how unpleasant your day was, with no carriage and no company. Mine was much worse, I assure you."

"You lost Henry's letter?" she asked, relegating it in importance several degrees below her own trying day.

"Its contents have been delivered to London."

"You evaded Kiley, then, did you? That troubled me as much as all the rest, worrying he had got hold of you."

"He did get hold of me. It was Colonel Landon's idea to take it to London instead of Ipswich. I agreed with him."

"Colonel Landon!" she spat out, then had recourse to a long draw from her vinaigrette. Her eyes watered from the pungent vapors of the smelling salts contained within. "I declare, these salts are years old. There is not a bit of power left in them. It is Landon who is to blame for the whole of our miseries."

"Did you not listen to what was said in the other room? It is Carlisle who is the spy."

"One is as bad as the other. It was not civil of Carlisle to enter my room when I was not there. He left the window open as well, to fill the room with that unhealthy night air. Whatever you have endured this day, Vanessa, it cannot hold a candle to my woes."

"If you would have preferred being kidnapped, drugged, stripped and tied up a prisoner to being without a carriage, then I wish we might have changed places."

"Stripped?" she asked, rising to a bolt upright position on her bed. "Which of the bounders did it? He must marry you."

"I don't know that it was done by a man at all. It might very well have been Mrs. Euston."

"Pray do not confuse me with any more names. If you were stripped by anyone but Mrs. Euston, the man must certainly marry you, and I hope you are not going to tell me it was Kiley. He'll beat you regularly."

"Colonel Landon is his name."

"So it *was* him. I might have known. If you are forced to marry that blackamoor, Vanessa, pray do not tell me you mean to make your home at Levenhurst, or I shall move direct to London."

"I am afraid you will be seeing Colonel Landon whether I marry him or not. He is replacing Forrester as the commanding officer at the local garrison."

"We are losing that nice Colonel Forrester? Oh, this is too much. And you never even got to stand up with him at the ball. I should not be the least surprised to learn Miss Fischer got an offer from him."

"I hope she did," Vanessa said, as the lady spoken of was a prime piece of competition.

"I knew how it would be when we had to miss the ball."

"There will be other balls."

"Not with Forrester at them. Well, Nessie, it seems to me you have done a poor job of accounting for yourself. Why did you leave me here all alone to deal with those scoundrels?"

The story was told, with many interruptions and animadversions from Miss Simons that the girl was not only ruined but depraved to have allowed herself to be used so poorly.

"The upshot of it is that you must marry one of them, to save your name from disgrace," she concluded.

"Marrying a spy would not do me much credit."

"I do not count on Landon to do the proper thing. He will try to squeak out of it by blaming it on Carlisle."

"Landon always does the proper thing," Vanessa answered hotly.

"Calling himself Kiley—is that your notion of proper, to be changing your name?"

"His name is Stanier Landon."

"Stanier? You never mentioned *that* before. Would he be one of the Dorchester Staniers?" she asked, swinging her legs over the side of the bed.

"Stanier is his Christian name, not the family name."

"Stanier is not a Christian name in the least. In fact, I believe it is French. You may rest assured it is his mama's family name. He is some kin to Jessica Stanier, certainly. He has a look of her about the eyes, now I come to think of it."

"He has very nice eyes," Vanessa said, in a pensive way.

"Yes, if you have a taste for gypsies."

"Who is Jessica Stanier?"

"Viscount Dorval's eldest daughter. Very good ton. She made her bows the year I did in London. She got picked off early in the season."

"Did she marry someone called Landon?"

"She must have," was the foolish answer. "If the colonel is Jessica Stanier's son, he is at least well bred. There must be some fortune there; Jessica had a good dot, whatever about the husband's fortune."

"It is not clear he is Jessica's son."

"Rubbish. Who else could he possible be? Stanier is not a common name. And he is coming home to take over command of the garrison there, you say?"

"Yes, but he will be delayed due to his injury. I hope it is not serious."

"Run along to his room and see what the doctor has to say. Go at once, goose, before some other chit snatches him away from you. Wait till I tell Mrs. Fischer. She'll be green with envy. Forrester to be fired, and Landon taking over in his stead. He is young to be a colonel, too. Henry was not promoted till he was fifty. Run along, before he changes his mind."

With a deep sense of alarm at this peculiar warning, Vanessa ran toward the door.

"Wait, come back, Nessie. You must not let him see you like that. You look a perfect nightmare. Your trunk is halfway to Scotland by now, but your small valise is still here. Why did you not take it with you? We shall try if we can make you half presentable, at least. There is no point thinking to attach Colonel Landon, looking like a witch."

The dame's migraine was forgotten. They got out the small valise, to repair the ravages of the day. Hot water was ordered for a bath, the hair was brushed and arranged, a russet sarsenet gown selected, appropriate jewelry discussed.

"Pearls are good for an invalid's room," Miss Simons said, cocking her head to one side to ponder her own pronouncement. "They have a *calming* quality, don't you think? I never wear a sparkling gem in a sickroom. It shows a lack of consideration."

Even this absurdity was accepted. "I shall go with you," Miss Simons declared, her face set in lines of concentration for the polite puzzle she was considering. "Ten minutes," she said, after due deliberation. "Ten minutes will be the proper duration of my visit. You may stay twenty—ten with me, ten alone with the colonel. As he is wounded, there can be no vice in it. He must have an opportunity to do the proper thing. Now, be sure you don't let him off the hook, Nessie."

"He is not on the hook," she answered, gliding to the mirror to assess the bait. The excitement lent a sparkle to her eyes. On her cheeks rode two rose spots that looked unnatural, but attractively so. She looked *different* somehow, in a subtle way she could not pinpoint. It was the expression of resolution that accounted for it, perhaps. She looked like a lady with a mission, one she did not intend to fail. That dreamy, irresolute, pouting face so admired by Forrester had taken on the first impression of character.

"Now, stop making faces in the mirror and *go*," Elleri ordered. "If he does not consider himself caught, I shall just put a little bug in his ear."

"No! You mustn't. *He* didn't do anything wrong. He

owes me nothing.'' Her blush heightened to recall certain parts of her story not told to Elleri. She had not said to what lengths Landon had gone in looking for the letter.

''Does he not? I should like to know why you are as pink as a rose, then,'' Miss Simons said sagely, and strode into the hallway.

The doctor had applied a plaster over Landon's left brow. It sat at an insouciant angle above the eye, giving him a quizzical air. His face was pale, but his eyes alert. He lay propped up in Miss Simons' bed, giving orders to the two stalwart officials. As the ladies entered, his eyes flew to Vanessa. He smiled, but the knowing Miss Simons did not find on him the smile of a lover. There was something of stiffness, constraint, that was far removed from a man on the verge of an offer. After debating with herself, she had found it possible to give Henry's tentative approval to the match.

''You can go now,'' Landon said to the men. ''I'll be in London tomorrow.''

''Not tomorrow,'' the doctor contradicted. ''One day of rest at the minimum. I insist.''

''Thank you, Doctor. You can go now too,'' Landon replied. After the doctor had clucked a few times and left, the colonel turned back to the officials. ''Tell Pitt I'll be in London by mid-afternoon tomorrow. You'd better leave right away, Easters. You stay at the jail, George, and make sure Carlisle and Euston are locked up right and tight, till I can get around to them.''

The elder gentleman was selected for the easier task of staying at the jail. Even that he had taken into consideration, Vanessa noticed, marveling at his thoroughness. She knew all the details of the Carlisle affair would be handled with equal efficiency. He would be interrogated, probably roughly, to discover what other spy activities he was involved in. The projected invasion would be handled by military and political experts. Her chore was done, but for the personal one of trying now to hook herself a husband. She had to convince Stanier she had changed, was not just a silly, selfish girl, but a woman, ready to face real life. She wanted that life to be at his side. He would demand much of Mrs. Landon—more than a pretty face and an ability to hold polite parties.

"Well, Colonel," Miss Simons said, walking briskly to the bedside. "What a pity you find yourself in this state. It will delay your doing what you must, and no doubt *want*, to do."

"It won't delay me long. I can be in London by tomorrow."

"It will be better to come down to Hastings with us as soon as you are able. You will want to speak to Colonel Bradford."

"I will, of course. He will have excellent advice to give me, but it must wait till I have made some arrangements in London."

"What sort of arrangements?" she asked, frowning. "Financial, do you mean?"

"That too. We shall require a good deal more funds than are presently available."

She smiled and nodded, happy to hear funds were available for a high life-style. "There is no reason you cannot stay with us at Levenhurst for the present. Of course you will want your own place eventually."

He blinked, looking from Miss Simons to her very embarrassed niece. "I will live at headquarters," he said.

"What about Vanessa?"

"I assume she will go on living with her father," he answered, mystified.

"Perhaps for a month or two," Miss Simons agreed, but not happily.

He began to understand the drift of the woman's questions and statements. A sly smile settled on his features as he leaned back against the pillows with a sigh of contentment to roast them.

"Longer than that, surely," he said.

"For how long have you in mind?" Elleri asked.

"Till she marries, probably."

"When will that be?"

"That is up to the lady."

"Well, Nessie, there you are!" Miss Simons said, beaming a smile of victory on her niece. "I told you he would

do the proper thing. You may set the date yourself."
Nessie rolled an angry, repressive eye at her aunt, who
was much too happy to see it.

"Tell me, Colonel, are you kin to Jessica Stanier, from
Dorchester? She would be your mama?"

"Why, no, she is my aunt. Do you know her?"

"Know her? We are old friends; we made our curtseys
together eons ago. Don't ask how long. So you are Jessica's nephew. What was your mama's name?"

"Estelle—she is Jessica's younger sister. Do you know
her too?"

"Well, now, that is very odd. I did not recall Jessica
had a sister. Your papa—who is he? Not that it *matters*,
my dear colonel. You hold the same rank as Henry Bradford, and at a much younger age. You will end up a
general, without a doubt." She smiled benignly, but kept
her ears open to hear who his father was too.

"Papa is Sir Charles Landon, from Surrey. Our home is
called Ashcliffe."

"Ashcliffe! I have seen it a dozen times in the books. It
is a famous old Gothic place."

"Queen Anne, actually."

"One of those periods. Your papa is a scientist, is he
not? I am sure I have read of his new contraption used in
mines."

"He is very much interested in horticulture. His new
strain of rose is often written up."

"Yes, so it was. Roses or engines—I knew I had read
something about him. It was the rose for which he was
knighted, was it not?" she asked, to pinpoint the "Sir"
more closely.

"My father is a baronet, as his ancestors have been for a
few centuries."

"I make sure he would have received a knighthood had
it not been for the baronetcy. Have you many brothers?"

"Just one, an *elder* brother, who will inherit Ashcliffe,"
he said, shattering her dreams of being able to call Nessa
"Lady Landon." "The only son seldom enters the Army,
you know," he pointed out, while his glance slid to Vanessa,
to gauge her reaction to his announcement. She was so

ashamed of her aunt's display that she looked quite discomfited.

"It is no matter. Vanessa will get Levenhurst, so you will always have a roof over your head." She considered the likelihood of Landon's being soon a general, of his father's baronetcy and the joy of showing Mrs. Fischer a picture of Ashcliffe, and accepted him.

"I shall leave you two alone now. Remember, Nessie, ten minutes. I doubt it will take that long," she added, with an arch and encouraging smile to the invalid.

Vanessa turned bright pink, and examined the farthest corner of the floor with a studious interest. Her aunt went at a lively gait out the door, to begin drawing up a list of wedding guests.

"You must not mind Auntie," was Vanessa's first humble speech. She rattled on to change the topic. "What does the doctor say? Did he have to remove a bullet?"

"No, it only grazed the skin. My skull was too hard to allow it to penetrate. I expect there is a bent bullet about the room somewhere, ruined from having collided with my head. You struck your blow at the wrong part of the anatomy when you attacked me with the clock."

"Where would be a more vulnerable spot?" she asked, trying to match his light tone. "I enquire in case I have to prevent you from ravishing me another time."

"The heart," he answered, with a bold smile. "Pull yourself up a chair, Vanessa. I am obliged to be as uncivil as ever in not doing it for you, but I hold my condition responsible. You must not blame it on the coarsening influence of the Army. The sawbones tells me I must not get up for a few hours."

"He said a day at the minimum," she reminded him, choosing to ignore his little taunt.

"I am too busy to malinger for more than eight hours, but I must have a little sleep. It begins to look as though a new embargo has been laid on me as well. I did not realize I was expected to make an honest woman of you, after your sufferings at Carlisle's hands."

"If I am ruined, then I prefer to remain so, rather than be redeemed by him."

"Of course I *did* add my mite. Did I ever apologize for ripping the dress off you?"

"I cannot imagine *how* you came to overlook anything. No, you did not, sir."

"I am sorry. At gunpoint is not my favorite way to undress a lady."

"Don't smirk like that. I'm not going to ask you what is."

"You'll see soon enough," he warned, reaching for her fingers. Whatever his way, she knew it would be efficient.

"My aunt is a foolish old lady. Pay no heed to her nattering. I don't."

"I have observed that unladylike strain of self-will in you. I believe I have—er, *mentioned* it."

"At some length. You were right."

"No, I was angry, and jealous as a green cow. I deserved to have my ears boxed for that boyish display of bad manners."

"There was some truth in it. I *was* raised badly, but not by Papa. He was seldom home. When he was, I was treated more strictly. He spanked me—once. It is recorded in Aunt Elleri's annals as the brutality of the decade. I was playing with some of his papers, and he turned me over his knee and gave me a good whopping."

"Not a bad chastisement. I have frequently felt the compulsion to do the same thing to you these past few days. Several other things as well," he added, pulling her up from the chair. He patted the edge of the bed, for her to sit beside him. She perched precariously on the edge of the mattress.

"I *did* behave like a child, but I have changed. The old Vanessa would not have gone after Carlisle—come here, I mean, to catch him. I really feel I have grown up—*matured*, I mean—remarkably in the last few days," she said earnestly, while he smiled fondly on her.

"Before this rapidly aging female turns gray on me, there was something else I wanted to do, besides spank you. I think you are just the right age for it now," he said, pulling her into his arms, to kiss her till her head spun. His fingers played on her neck, stroking her hair, then caressing her cheeks, as she drew away from him. With a slight pressure, he pulled her back. "Don't go yet. That was just for the bullet. You still owe me for the clock." He kissed her again, with a gentle passion that surprised her. She was beguiled by this gentleness in a violent man.

"I am not always a vicious brute, you know," he said. "A soldier needs a wife more than most men, to refine and—subdue him—his wilder nature, I mean."

"I don't want to be just a refinement in your life, Stanier. A diversion, I mean."

"My sweetest heart, diversion is the only enjoyable part of our life in the military. We don't *like* killing our fellowmen, contrary to popular opinion. You will prevent my becoming a boor, and I will prevent your diverting any other officer but me. How's that for a good bargain on *my* part?" he asked, laughing at his selfishness.

"It sounds fine to me," she said happily.

"Me too. Divert me, Vanessa."